The Drake Odyssey

The Drake Odyssey

James G Ralls

authorHOUSE®

AuthorHouse™
1663 Liberty Drive
Bloomington, IN 47403
www.authorhouse.com
Phone: 1-800-839-8640

First published by AuthorHouse   11/11/2011

ISBN: 978-1-4670-5239-9 (sc)
ISBN: 978-1-4670-5237-5 (hc)
ISBN: 978-1-4670-5229-0 (ebk)

Library of Congress Control Number: 2011918199

Printed in the United States of America

CONTENTS

THE AMBIANCE... 1

SMOKE!!... 3

THE RESCUE 7

THE DEPUTIES 10

THE SHERIFF.. 16

UNCLE CLINT 21

THE MOUNTAIN 29

THE PROFESSOR 41

DRAKE 48

THE DAY 55

THE LONG HAUL 57

THE MOMENT!... 63

THE MORNING 66

NORMAN ROCKWELL, SAWDUST AND CAT........................... 74

IT IS UNCLE CLINT!... 88

RETURN TO THE MOUNTAIN 92

THE MUSEUM.. 98

ABOUT THE AUTHOR.. 107

ABOUT THE BOOK 109

DEDICATION

I leave this short novel to my children and grandchildren in hopes that it may give them some insight as to what occurs and goes on in the mind of their father and grandfather.

THE AMBIANCE

Dragonflies and hummingbirds skim and dart around the flowers of my garden, not unlike the children of our county fair who rush to the corn dog and cotton candy vendors. All want the sweetness and flavor of tastes that satisfy and quench all of our insatiable desires.

And indeed, I am not unlike the children and dragonflies and humming birds, for I desire the cool sweet, snow-melted waters that pour over my hot and worn-out feet that have taken me over miles of hard terrain to reach this almost cathedral place in the high Sierras. It has been a long and difficult trek to reach this point. I enjoy this sensation! A sensation of aches and pain earned by the toil and sweat of exploring sights and scenes that some may only ever see in travel magazines and documentary films. And why not enjoy these sensations? I am old, by most of today's standards. But it is good that I am now retired and have the time to enjoy these long treks that I once made as a young man in the mountains of New Mexico. These young people's ideas of fun and adventure run contrary to mine. I find my personal achievements and goals of mind over body to be greater than mind over a computer game or contest of wit and skill.

Well, for the moment, the cool waters of the high Sierras are cooling my feet; my camp is ready for the night. And I have prepared the canned chunk white chicken, mustard, crackers and canned mandarin oranges for my evening meal. The sun setting in the west has prepared the perfect evening with scarlet skies and a cool breeze to chill my tent. Ahh! The ambiance! I have a good life!

Evening falls, my vision of the skies are almost blurred by older eyes that see the stars in duplicate. But, instead of a five-star hotel tonight, I enjoy a room with at least a million stars. And, indeed, I have a good life.

Sleep, deep wonderful sleep, so uncommon to many of us. Shameful that it escapes us so often. But on that one and so infrequent occasion that it does happen to us, it is so wonderful. We have to get away from all that bothers us to enjoy it. And here, in that almost magical, almost elusive, and almost impossible moment, it happened to me. A quiet wonderful night of sleep! But the awakening was horrid!

SMOKE!!

No! I did not light a fire! But I smell smoke! And voices, loud voices, unfriendly voices! Quickly, I reach for the zipper of my bag and reach for my boots and pants! My experiences in the military and Viet Nam still cause me to prepare to be ready to go at a moment's notice! All that I need is ready and by my side! Clothing, boots, knife, and that unused and untested Colt 45 that I carry to ward off that very old mountain lion or bear—too old to hunt for its usual quarry and may want an unsavory and unusual human being for lunch! I am ready in just moments! But this is not wild animals that I am concerned about! Animals do not light a fire! And, as for humans? Who in their right mind would light a fire here in the high Sierras with the fire danger so high?

I listen, and I wait. Those sounds and scents are coming from over the granite rocks that I slept underneath last night! And the sounds—are those of anger and torture. I have heard those sounds before in Viet Nam. The interrogation of prisoners! Damn! Memories blocked out for years are suddenly flooding over me as I listen to behavior and violence that is incomprehensible. I dare to look over the granite and witness the scene. Three men are looking down on the prostate figure of an old man! Cursing and kicking him, they are exhorting him to talk! But talk about what?

"Screw you, you old man! You are not faking a heart attack on me! Get up and keep going or you'll die right here!" Words spoken by a tall blonde-haired man who is stepped back, but apparently in control of the other two men who are with him.

Another man, shorter than the tall blonde, but of significant size and stature, looks over the tortured body of the old man on the ground. He is stout, shaved head, and every bit the look of someone you would not want to encounter. Perhaps a retired boxer or professional wrestler that took an easier job than performing for the public. His fists are clinched. Fists of stone! And then he reaches down, grabs the old man by the throat, lifts him, and, yes! The fists of stone resonate against the Sierras as he drives them into the old man's body! Oh, God!

I cringe, and drop to my knees behind the granite. A coward I am! What can I do? So, I listen. The torture goes on. Suddenly, I stand and with that untested Colt 45, walk suddenly toward the trio of torturers! What in hell am I doing? One lesson of combat is that you never go into combat with an untested weapon. This old 45 has not been fired in decades! After Viet Nam, I swore that I would never raise a weapon against any living thing again. But suddenly I find myself raising that weapon in the air and pulling the trigger! It fired! And just as suddenly and surprisingly to the trio of torturers, I have the muzzle of that old reliable Colt 45 in the face of the tall blonde man.

They are more stunned than I am! Here in the high country of the Sierras, they thought they were alone in their misdeeds and torture of this old man lying at their feet.

I closed the distance between them and myself purposefully! Pull your enemy up to your belt buckle as quickly as possible. If you retreat, you are in their kill zone! How did they not know I was camped so close to them? My targets are already selected. The tall blonde facing the muzzle of my Colt 45, the shaved-headed fists of stone captured in my peripheral vision, the mouse-faced man with sharp-pointed nose also in my vision. But the point of my attack is the tall blonde man who is so obviously in control of the others. 'Hope to hell I am right!! And I am constantly and continually looking into his eyes!

"Thor?" the shaved-headed man says. Obviously, awaiting a command to attack me!

"Tell your dog to stand down or your blonde-headed scalp will be scattered all over these mountains!" I say with as clear and authoritative voice as I can raise to the blonde-headed man.

I am standing in front of him. Close enough to have him fully locked in my sights, but just far enough away to avoid his swinging his arms to knock my weapon away or swinging out to attack me.

He is blonde, but not a dumb blonde. He knows this is his moment of decision!

"Lucas, do not do anything. Let's see what this man has to say," says Thor.

Thor? What kind of name is that? What kind of parent would give that name to a kid? Either he was born to a couple in the '70s or he is Scandinavian. I'll give him the latter of the two choices.

"Well, Thor, since we are playing Simon Says, Simon says to all of you to sit down and take off your boots!"

"Do it right now!!" I demand.

Damn! It is hard to keep us this tone of authority and control. My heart is on fire and racing as well as my mind!

Once again, Lucas calls out, "Thor?"

"Shut up Lucas and do as he says!"

Perhaps Thor recognizes his predicament because I had paused long enough before this assault for the morning dew and fog to collect on my Colt 45 so as to cause thin, gray wisps of steam to rise from the hot muzzle that is locked between his eyes! I see them rising, and so must he!

They sit down and as they do, I yell out, "Keep your hands out in front of you and do not, and I absolutely mean, do not, make any sudden moves!"

My eyes have been scanning the scene. Thank goodness that I have good peripheral vision. It appears that they had been so confident that they were alone in their misdeeds that their handguns had been left close to their sleeping gear, out of reach for now. Do I have good luck and good timing, or what? They were so focused on the beating and torture of the old man that they paid no attention to what was around them. The deep sleep that I had so dearly enjoyed last night could have been disastrous if they had known of my close proximity to them last night. Yeah, I must be leading a good life.

"Now, get on your feet!" I yell out to the sock-clad trio. "Okay, now, Thor, have your mouse-faced friend there gather up those boots and throw them in the fire!" Thor hesitates, and as I thrust the muzzle slightly closer to his face, he tells Ugly to do so. The mouse does so.

"Now, head down that slope, keep going, and do not look back!" Simply thought, this horrible trio's feet will be torn to shreds after a few hundred yards of granite rock and stones. If they do try to pursue me, I will be able to put yards and miles between them and me in very short time.

Thor decides to get defiant! "Are you nuts?" he yells out. "What makes you think you can get away from us? We will round back and be on you in no time!"

"Well, Thor, if you do not get away from here soon, the authorities will be here and I will not worry about you rounding back. They have been called."

"Well, Simon, or whatever your name is, your bluff is being called. No authorities have been called, for you are well out of cell phone range and no one is coming to rescue you or this old fool!" Thor is right about part of his challenge.

"Thor, you are right! There is no cell phone service up here, but I did not call them! You and your idiots did! That smoking fire you built of wet and green wood called them!"

"The forest service guards these forests like the Beefmasters of the Tower of London watch after the Queen's jewelry. Believe me, there are smoke jumpers and fire crews on their way here right now!"

And in only moments, I witness the once again stunned look in his eyes in that he knew I was right.

"So, Thor, I suggest that you and Lucas, and whatever name that shriveled up mouse you have with you is, start making your way down this mountain."

Thor, without a word in response, turned, motioned for his cohorts in torture to follow him, and started making a tender bare-footed way down the mountain.

THE RESCUE

Oh, thank God! I was right! No sooner than they had disappeared into the forests far below than I hear the faint whoop-whoop of a helicopter's incoming flight. 'Could not tell the direction of flight, for I had not been able to look away from the trio of torturers line in flight. Although not the familiar sound of the Hueys of Viet Nam, it was definitely a helicopter coming for our rescue!

And now, I look down at the old man for whom this moment had occurred. Was I wrong in what I have just done? Perhaps the old man was the real culprit in this moment. Were Thor and his companions the ones whom I should have been supporting? Judgments made without knowledge and forethought are often wrong. No! I must rely on instinct in times like this. I think, I hope, I made the right judgment of action.

Oh, my! The elevation here is at least 7,000 feet and far removed from any established roads or four-wheeled drive trails. This old man is not suited for this terrain's demands. Khaki-clad with a light shirt and shoes fit only for a casual neighborhood or shopping mall stroll. Not a portly man, but certainly someone who only enjoys a good and soft life of gentle demeanor and even softer exercise. What could he be doing at such an altitude and rough demands? Not here by choice, that is for sure.

He looks up at me and is wheezing and clutching his chest. He seems to more worried about his chest than the bruising and swelling on his face. One eye is already almost fully swollen shut and the older skin on his arms is bruised. The skin on one arm is torn and bleeding. But I see no major blood loss except to his head. But even slight head wounds bleed profusely. I know they are generally are not fatal. Quickly, and with desperation, I am trying to recall the immediate care action to be given to a wounded comrade in action. Damn! Decades have passed, and all I can remember is to stop the bleeding, compress the wounds, and loosen the clothing! He is breathing, so no resuscitation of any kind is required. But what about his wheezing and clutching of his chest? Damn! He really is having a heart attack! This, I am not prepared for! He is trying to talk. I tell him to just be quiet, not to talk, and remind him that help is on the way!

The helicopter has found us and is hovering just above. I stand and wave and point down at the old man. The quiet spell of the Sierra high country is replaced with screams of man and machine!

Out of the chopper and on a dropped line is what appears to be tools and gear and suddenly behind it drops a man repelling down a line. He drops suddenly and is soon on the ground. Damn! Decades before, I had done the similar drop out of a Huey and, oh my geez! This is too vivid a memory! Damn! I've got to control my emotions now. Do not go back there! This is now, and this old man needs us in control of the moment.

I collect my thoughts and the well-muscled-toned man out of the chopper makes his way towards us. If he is a smoke jumper, surely he has been trained in first responder aid and can render better aid than I can to this old man. I hope he can, for now I feel helpless towards the care of this old man. It is obvious that the jumper is making immediate observation of the situation before him. He looks to me, then to the old man and the billowing smoke from the campfire.

I smell the scent of boots burning! Not what I should be concerned about at this moment.

The jumper walks right up to my face and nose to nose and over the noise of the chopper, says something, all of which I cannot understand, but I gather that he is asking about what the situation is here.

I respond, "I think he is having a heart attack!" I point to the old man. "And I think someone was trying to kill him."

The jumper looks to the old man and then at the campfire. Obviously his training has focused on fire control, but he seems to realize the priorities of the moment and looks skyward to the chopper hovering above. His words over his mike to the chopper are drowned out to me. The chopper begins to move towards what appears to be a more suitable landing spot on the slope. It begins to land.

The jumper is kneeled down over the old man. I look around at the campsite and begin to gather things, especially the weapons left behind by the trio of torturers.

The jumper stands, and with a note of authority and surety in his voice, tells me to help him take the old man to the chopper that has landed just beneath the campsite. Oh, thank God for someone like this jumper who seems to be so full of youth and authority, for I am not doing well at this moment.

Together, the jumper and I drag the old man to the chopper. And then I ask to go back to the campsite to gather the weapons and other gear I had assembled. It just seems foolish to leave such things behind for the trio to round back and have them once again. I get no argument from the jumper and together we gather them and threw them on the floor of the chopper. We lifted, and, oh so sweet, we left that scene of horror.

THE DEPUTIES

The jumper remains kneeled over the old man and is communicating with the pilot. Their words are drowned out to me by the sound of blades and an engine that is working hard to lift and carry us through the thin air of these high peaks. I know nothing about this craft's capabilities at this altitude and I can only guess that the cool heavy air of morning is a good thing at the moment. I can only assume that the pilot and jumper are going straight to a hospital and their only concern at the moment is time, speed and distance. It is good to be in what seems to be capable and professional care. I've been doing a lot of guessing over the past few minutes! Has it only been minutes? Seems like a life time and despite one of the best nights of sleep I have enjoyed in years, I am totally exhausted!

Suddenly, I have just realized I left all my gear at my campsite!

Seems like a small loss compared to the near and still possible loss of the old man's life, I know; but, being retired, if I have to replace that gear, it's going take a big hunk out my fixed income. Damn. Suddenly I find myself feeling selfish for having these thoughts about my gear while the old man is fighting for his life.

As we rush in flight over the vast conifer forests and granite peaks, I am in awe of this magnificent view below us. Suddenly I am lost in memories of what it was like in flight over the jungles and rice paddies of South Viet Nam. Too many events this morning have caused old memories to resurface, and I absolutely do not like this day. I've got to get back to the present. This day has only begun.

We have passed over the high peaks, and there is only the forest below us now. Roads are meandering through the canyons below and I see glimpses of homes and other buildings below us. We are beginning our descent. I see our landing site now and there are flashing blue and red lights atop three vehicles. One looks to be an ambulance; and, yes, the others must be law enforcement.

As we land and the pilot cuts power to the chopper, we are approached by three people who must be the paramedics. I stay still on my seat as they immediately start examining the old man and assessing his condition. Professionals are at work, and I can't help but admire their commitment to their job. One suddenly turns to me and orders me out. I go quickly!

I hit the ground, and no sooner than I look up, there are what appear to be county deputies in my face. I am startled!

"Sir, do you need medical attention?" questions one of the deputies.

"No," I respond.

"Then please come with us." And he steps back and points toward his squad car.

"But what about him?" as I point towards the old man just being brought out of the chopper.

"He is in good hands and is being taken to the hospital." His voice most definitely is one of genuine authority.

"But isn't a deputy going to accompany him to the hospital?" I ask.

"And why should a deputy accompany him, sir?" Now suspicion is interlaced in his authoritative voice.

"Some people have just tried to kill him only a short time ago, and I am afraid they might try again." I am beginning to get nervous now. I can hear the quivering in my voice.

The deputy pauses, looks to his partner and says to him, "Ben, stay with the victim."

With that said, my nerves begin to calm and I start walking to the squad car. Before I get to the car, the deputy orders me to halt. Suddenly, I am really nervous again. I just remembered that the muzzle of that Colt 45 had cooled and I had stuck it in my waist band and had pulled my sweater over the handle.

The deputy speaks out again," Sir, I am going to ask you to put your hands on the hood of the car, spread your legs. I am going to search you and cuff you before I put you in the car."

It is time for me to speak up. "Officer, I have a 45 in my front waistband. And I have a large knife on my belt." I waste no time in telling him about old reliable.

And now the deputy pulls his weapon and I feel his heightened sense of caution.

With my hands on the squad car and feet spread wide, the deputy reaches around and pulls old reliable out of my waist band. And then, he takes my knife.

"Thank you for warning me, Sir. It is best you did. Does this Colt 45 belong to you?"

"Yes." But I respond weakly for I knew I was in trouble now, for the weapon was not registered. I had purchased it not long after my military discharge and release from Walter Reed Hospital back in 1969. It was easy to buy a handgun then. It was simply cash and carry. The only time I had fired the weapon was the one time I went to a range and put a couple of magazines of ammo through it. Other than that, I had only cleaned it enough to keep the dust and rust off. It may have saved the old man's life, and possibly mine, today; but now; I can only fear the legal problems I may now face. I'm looking at concealed weapon, no permit, no registration. Damn! Now I fear more costs and problems. This is not a good day.

The deputy is reading me my Miranda rights as he is cuffing me. Just before he puts me in the squad car, the ambulance leaves with the other deputy's car leading the way. Oh, well, I am better off than the old man. At least I am not lying on a gurney with IVs in my veins. But as the deputy seats me in the back of the squad car, I begin to doubt if I am any better off than the old man. The cuffs are tight and hurting my wrists. Why do they put these hard plastic seats in the back of these squad cars? Perhaps it is because they are harder to damage by some of the unwilling that they put back here. In any event, this is not a very comfortable ride that I am taking right now.

The ride to wherever we are going seems to be taking us right through town. There are historic-appearing buildings that seem to house boutique and antique shops, bakeries and coffee shops. All have historic facades that speak of frontier days of old. The bars and dance halls that come right out of the 1800s certainly emphasize the historic theme. All are definitely seeking the tourist trade dollars. And now, we are driving through what must be the residential area. Row houses that have steeped pitch roofs, white picket fences, all accompanied by at least one fruit tree and a garden on the side. This was at one time a company town of the old lumber and timber when lumber manufacturing was king; and the king owned the town, houses, the company store, the sawmill, and all who worked there. Oh, my, how times have changed.

We finally reach our destination. It is a somewhat more modern-appearing building; but by modern, I only mean that it does not have a frontier façade. Probably built in the '70s or '80s of concrete and cinder blocks plastered over with what seems a new coat of paint. Other squad cars are parked all about us as we pull around the back and go through a gated fence. He is taking me in through the back door. I don't even deserve a front door entry. Now, I really feel like a common criminal.

We enter the building and am told to take off my shoes and a different deputy pats me down again, takes my wallet, my ball point pen, and asks me if I have anything on me that could be used as a weapon. I just stare at him and shake my head, no.

"Sir," the deputy says. "I need a verbal response."

"No," I say aloud, and now I am really beginning to feel annoyed. But then, I try to calm myself by realizing that they are just adhering to standard procedure that assures control of a prisoner and assures them of their safety. But it is difficult not to take this humiliating procedure personally.

And all at once, I recognize how all these deputies moving about all look the same! They all seemed to be cloned! All well-muscle toned, short cropped hair, all about six feet to six feet, three inches. They all have stone-sculpted jaws and chins, and voices that are not mono-toned, but certainly strong voices that ring with authority. I think I may have difficulty distinguishing the deputy that brought me here from the others!

I am told to sit down in a chair beside a small table. Another deputy enters the room and sits down at the table. Oh, thank goodness! This deputy is a woman! At least I will be able to distinguish her from the others. She also is well toned and possesses a voice of control and authority. Do they send all these deputies to speech therapy to learn how to have so much authority and control in their voices? Or perhaps it is a result of their training and the confidence they have in themselves and this organization. I think it is the latter.

"I am going to ask you a few questions, Sir, and I need verbal responses. Do you understand me, Sir?"

"Yes." I respond, and now I notice that all have been courteous thus far, but are most definitely in control of me.

And she begins to ask questions about any drugs or alcohol that I may have recently ingested. Am I on any prescribed medications? To which I start citing a number of prescriptions, many of which I have abandoned at my campsite.

Okay, so I know that this is all standard procedure, but I am tired of the process. And then, I am given a pair of paper slippers to wear and taken down to another desk where another cloned deputy takes my photo, fingerprints me and asks me if I would have any difficulty if I were placed in a cell with an African-American, Hispanic or any other race than white.

"Huh! No!" I yell out. "What in the hell is the reason for that question? Now I have had enough. I have Hispanics, African Americans, and East Indians for neighbors down in the valley. And we all get along just fine. I resent the suggestion that I may be racist and am offended by such a question! And, furthermore, why in the hell am I going to be placed in a cell? I haven't hurt anyone and no one has even asked me what the hell happened up there in the high country!"

"Calm down, Sir. Unfortunately Sir, many of our inmates do have difficulty because of racist attitudes, and we ask this so only as to avoid disturbances in our jail. Now, first, you will be placed in a holding cell by yourself, but someone will be arriving soon who will give you an opportunity to explain what has happened to you." The deputy has maintained his demeanor in spite of my outburst. And having heard his explanation, I understand the logic of his question. I calm down.

I am taken down a hallway and placed into a small cell of concrete walls. There is a very bright light overhead and a thin, plastic-covered pad on a concrete platform that serves as a bed. No pillow. A stainless steel toilet and washbasin are in one corner of the room. No windows. The door is heavy steel, with a small narrow window and a small slot. A small plastic tray is passed through the slot almost as soon as the door is locked. On it is a steaming hot pocket sandwich and a squeezebox container of juice.

"'Thought you might be hungry, Sir." The clone says. I take it and place it on the floor. For some reason, I have lost all sense of hunger. It must be because of the lack of ambiance.

Whoever is in charge of this place must have some high standards and expectations that demand order and discipline, for this is a very efficient organization and cadre of officers.

THE SHERIFF

I do not know how much time has passed, for they have taken my watch, cell phone, wallet, and everything else personal, placed them in a plastic bag. They told me I would get them back should I be released. 'Even took my belt. I wear clothes a size too big when I trek in the woods so as to be loose and comfortable. I find myself tugging my pants back up because of the looseness of my waistband. Damn, do I feel uncomfortable!

Someone is at the cell door.

"Sir, step up to the door with your back side to it, place your hands to your backside so I may place cuffs on you." A clone is at my cell door.

I do so.

He cuffs me and says, "The sheriff and an investigator are going to speak to you and I am going to move you down to another room."

Thank goodness! Now maybe all can be explained and I can get out of here, I say to myself!

With cuffs on and the issued paper slippers on my feet, I shuffle down the hallway with the strong hand of the deputy on my arm.

Another door is opened. The deputy removes the cuffs. I shuffle in and a man in shirt and tie directs me to a chair in the corner by a small table and tells me to sit.

Someone else is standing in the corner of the small and brightly lit room. At first, I thought it to be another clone. But no, this clone is at least a full foot shorter than the rest. Perhaps only five-foot—two or—three, no more than a hundred ten pounds, and female. She appears to in her mid '30s to early '40s. She has small features and lacks the sculpted strong jaw and strong chin of the other clones. But she is wearing the freshly starched and nicely creased uniform of the other clones. Like the others, the uniform clings tightly to her body and reveals an obviously muscle toned body that is no stranger to a gym and its weight room. Everything about her is feminine, yet she retains and emits an aura about her that she is a professional officer of the law and is not to be taken lightly. The woman has a pretty face, but her demeanor is of someone to be reckoned with.

"Good evening, Mr. Becker." The man in coat and tie says.

"Mr. Becker, I know it has been a long day for you. Is there any thing that you need? Are you hungry, or do you need any type of medication? I see quite a list of medications that you told our deputy that you take."

The courteous question almost stuns me!

"No, no," I respond. "I can go for a while without the medications, and the lack of ambiance has stolen my appetite. But thank you for asking."

My eyes cannot help but look again at the officer in the corner.

"Well, Mr. Becker, I am Detective Jake Humphries, and the person behind me is Sheriff Huntsmen. We would like to ask you a few questions about what happened up on the mountain and offer you a chance to explain the events as you experienced them. Would you have a problem with that?"

Stunned again I am! Sheriff? That small-framed person that is standing to the back and left of you is the sheriff and the one responsible for all the clones and this tight-fitted ship that has so professionally dragged me through this process?

I come back to the question and respond. "No problem, Detective. I will gladly answer your questions and explain what happened if it can get me home."

"First, Mr. Becker, I understand that you have been told your Miranda rights but I am going to tell them to you again." And he did.

"Before you begin, Detective, I have a question for you. The old man who was so badly beaten . . . is he okay?"

The detective looks back to the sheriff who slightly nods, yes.

Yes, I say to myself. She not only has control, but also the respect of this investigator.

"What is his condition?" I ask further.

The detective looks back towards the sheriff who slightly nods, yes, again.

"Mr. Becker, there are patients' and victims' rights that we must safeguard, but I can tell you that he is in critical care. It is touch and go at the moment." Closely guarded words are at best spoken by the detective.

"Well," I say, "Considering the last few moments I spent with him, I guess that is the best I could hope for him. He was in bad shape the last time I saw him."

And the interrogation begins!

Have I ever been know by any aliases? Have I ever been arrested or suspected of any crime? Have I ever been fired from any job for any cause? Did I know or have I ever seen the victim before? Did I know or have I ever seen the alleged perpetrators before? What was I doing on the mountain? Describe the alleged perpetrators in detail. He asks these and other endless questions that seem unimportant to me but must have some purpose for the investigator to be asking them. The interrogation goes on and on. And the sheriff just stands there with an occasional nod or shake of the head. The investigator looks back when I occasionally respond with a question of my own.

Finally! I am asked to explain the event that took place on the mountain! And I recount every moment of the horror to them in exacting detail. I am done with the story. And the detective and sheriff look at one another.

Amazingly, after spending what seems like hours in silence behind her investigator, the sheriff speaks to me.

"Mr. Becker, why would the professor tell us over and over again that we must protect you?"

These words startle me so as to cause me to suddenly straighten up and back into my chair. I almost tumble backwards!

"The old man is a professor?" I say to myself.

"I'm sorry, Sheriff. What professor? I don't know any professor." I blurt out.

"I'm speaking of Professor Hubert Shumway of UC Berkeley," the sheriff says. "The man whose life you saved. At least he has been saved for the moment." The sheriff speaks in that clear and authoritative voice that all the deputies of her office possess.

I try to refocus on the question.

My words stumble. "I have no idea why he may have said that. Are you sure he was speaking about me? I have never seen the man until this morning."

"Yes, Mr. Becker. He clearly meant you."

Damn, for such a delicate-faced woman, her words punch with a thud of confidence and authority.

"Sheriff, I am clueless. I really am." I meekly respond.

The sheriff speaks again. "Mr. Becker, fortunately for you, we had an opportunity to speak with Professor Shumway, and he confirmed your story. So, for the time being, we are going to release you from the jail but ask that you stay in town for a few days. We are going to seek more information from you, so do not go out of town."

Oh, thank goodness! I am getting out of this place! But then an embarrassing thought races into my mind! And so, I mutter meekly.

"Sheriff, I am embarrassed to say it, but I am retired and on a fixed income. The cost of a hotel and meals bought out would really put a dent into my budget. I really appreciate being released, but couldn't I just go down to my home in the valley and drive back up here if you need me?"

She looks at me with what I interpret to be a look of understanding and tells me to follow her.

I follow her and the detective out of the interrogation room, down the hall, and into a room where a deputy hands me a plastic bag with my boots and other personal items in it. All is present but my Colt 45 and knife. He asks me to count the money in the wallet and asks if everything I had when I was processed into the jail is present. I tell him that it is, and he hands me an inventory sheet to sign. There is no use in mentioning my Colt 45 and knife, I am sure.

We leave the room and go up an elevator and into a room filled with desks occupied by people all seemingly busy. The sheriff's appearance seems to cause everyone in the room to straighten their backs and heighten their attention to their work. Her presence commands respect without words to demand it.

Oh, yeah, this is definitely the sheriff!

UNCLE CLINT

"Madge," the sheriff politely calls out to one of the women at a desk. "Call Lizzy down at the hotel and tell her to set a room aside for a few days. We'll be sending a guest down and tell her that his meals are also to be billed to the department."

Madge picks up the phone and dutifully responds.

"Mr. Becker, the hotel you are going to be put up in is down the street, about two blocks. You are to stay there until we call on you, which will probably be early morning. I just ask that you stay away from the steaks on the menu and spend county money as carefully as if it were your own. As per Professor Shumway's request, we are going to place a plains clothes officer in the hotel 24/7 and have a patrol car check out the hotel every hour."

"And, by the way, Mr. Becker, there are weapon violations still pending against you, so do not do anything stupid," she adds.

She goes on, "Officer Bentley will accompany you to the hotel."

For some reason, I think this goes beyond, for reasons I cannot fathom, the normal procedure of being courteous to a potential crime scene witness. What in the hell kinda mess have I gotten myself into?

"Thank you, Sheriff." I say and follow Deputy Bentley out of the building. I guess it would be foolish to ask if I could have my old reliable Colt 45 back now. So, I just follow the lead of the clone.

Darkness of night is falling against the streets, and the street lights are flickering on. The hotel that we are approaching is of at least forties vintage and has a historic façade that welcomes guests and seems to promise a most wonderful evening of comfort and respite from their day's long travel to arrive here. As we enter, the large doors are hung on

21

oversized hinges. Welcoming creaks usher us in. The carpet is overly plush, with broad deep forest green and brown prints of curled vines and flowers that lend a splashing of yellows and reds to the lush padding beneath our feet. The heavy carpeting cushions our heavy steps into silence, and the interior design is that of frontier antiques that can only be found at heavy market value in antique stores and boutiques. Heavy and darkly stained bookshelves line the walls of the lobby and shelve what appears to be a large collection of old and worn texts. An elderly couple is sitting on plush vintage chairs in the reading room with books on their laps that must be of Hemingway or Twain discourse. Nothing else would be appropriate for this setting. Their focus is on their reading, and our arrival does not disturb them in the least. The hotel desk is at our front. On our left appears to be a formal dining room whose tables are covered with fine, white linen. The silverware appears to be a collection mismatch of antique ware of sterling silver. At the extreme far side is a full frontier-style bar stocked with the finest liquors and beers. To the right is a country cafe with a swinging, gated entrance. Wafting over the gate and flowing into the lobby are warm aromas of steaming coffee and oh, such sweet smelling pies. Apple pie, I think. The place has quiet a nice setting. Nice ambiance.

"Hello, Lizzy," Deputy Bentley calls out. "We have a guest for you this evening."

"Oh, yes, David," says the mature and attractive figure behind the lobby desk. "And we have his room ready and table set if he would like to sit for dinner."

Deputy Bentley looks at me and asks, "Dinner first, Mr. Becker?"

The courtesies that these clones extend amaze me, but again, my appetite has been stolen from me by the day's events. All I want is a hot shower and bed, so I beg.

"Oh no, just a room and shower is all I want for the evening." Lizzy reaches down for the keyboard of a computer that seems out of place in this historic setting as Deputy Bentley recites all the data she requests.

Deputy Bentley escorts me up two flights of stairs. Each step has its unique sound of groans and squeaks. Again, the carpet is heavy but cannot hide the sounds of time's toll on the stairs.

I take the heavy key issued to me and open the door. Deputy Bentley puts his hand on my chest, pushes me back a bit and enters first. He enters, surveys the immediate interior, and then motions me in. He opens the closet doors and searches for what, I do not know. He looks in all corners and behind all the furniture. He opens the balcony curtains, steps out and looks all about. His surveillance of my room reeks of professional experience, but, as of this moment, I feel in peril. Again, I think. What have I exposed myself to in my action towards intervening in the old mans torture? Deputy Bentley's act of professionalism has only heightened my imagined fears!

I have no clean clothes for tomorrow. They were all left behind in my camp. But no sooner than I had these thoughts than Lizzy enters the door with clean denim jeans, a shirt, and clean underpants and a tee-shirt. Socks, even! All neatly folded and placed on my bed. Along with a razor and other needed condiments. All welcome indeed.

"The sheriff's department sent these down for you, Mr. Becker, and said if they do not fit then please let them know." Lizzy spoke as she placed them on the bed.

The courtesies of Sheriff Huntsmen's department amaze me even further. All pieces of clothing seem to be an exact fit. Lizzy hands me a plastic bag for my dirty clothes and tells me that if I place it on the door hook, they will washed and pressed. What great service!

But, again, I think. This all goes beyond what an ordinary crime scene witness might otherwise be extended.

My fear is heightened!

Deputy Bentley leaves, but in doing so says, "I will remain close by, Mr. Becker, until a plain clothes officer is in the hotel. Have a good night's sleep and good luck to you, Mr. Becker."

And with that, the clone leaves.

A hot shower, a shave, a quick brushing of my teeth, and between the sheets I dive!

But immediate sleep eludes me! So much unlike last night in my cool tent, with only a bag on a thin mat. I toss and turn, and with every toss and turn, I recount all of the events of the day. Failing to escape the thoughts, I try to escape them by recalling all of the good things in my life. My children, grandchildren, my retirement, and not having to experience the drudgery of the daily grind of having quotas and expectations of clients, managers, and employees that used to hound me every day.

But, to no avail, I have difficulty falling to sleep. Finally, fatigue conquers my concerns and I sleep. But, my sleep is fitful.

Bacon! I smell bacon! Oh, goodness, I sound like a dog food commercial. But, yes, my alarm clock is the smell of bacon!

Out of bed! Another hot shower and shave, and I throw on the clean clothes that the sheriff's department sent me and dash down the two flights of stairs. At the foot of the stairs, I, regain my composure and slowly stroll into the café of the hotel. The hunger strike that my body imposed on me yesterday is overcome by the scent of bacon and biscuits, coffee, and all the savory scents of a country breakfast!

I try to control the drooling in my mouth and sit down at the counter where three older men are sitting. They sound as though they are discussing politics, the weather and their last visit to their doctors, appropriate subjects for men of their age and experience. A waitress places a cup of coffee and menu in front of me before I am seated on the cushion of the antique high back chair.

Everything on the menu interests me and my eyes linger on steak and eggs that is so wonderfully described in the menu.

"Honey," the waitress says to me, "everything on the menu is great. Let me know when you are ready and I'll be back."

I watch her leave to serve her other customers, and suddenly I remember the sheriff's asking me to be careful with county money. So, I decide on the $3.99 bacon-and-egg special with country potatoes and biscuit. I call the waitress back over and she takes my order. As I drool and wait for my order, I cannot help but listen in on the loud voices and laughter of the older men at the counter.

The waitress places my order in front and says loud enough for all to hear.

"Aren't you the feller that the sheriff sent down here last night?"

Suddenly, the conversation and laughter of the older men stop and all eyes are focused on me.

"Yes," I quietly respond.

"Well, welcome to the hotel! If you are a friend of our sheriff, then you are a friend to all of us."

"Thank you,." I respond. And with that, the waitress returns to her other customers.

I nod my head toward the three older men at the counter. Their eyes are still settled on me. Their sudden silence makes me uneasy.

The man sitting closest to me speaks out. He appears to be in his early 70s, with a slender build and sliver hair that is thin, and his face is tanned. But he moves and speaks as a younger man would. No signs of old age on his body. His movements are fluid and his voice strong and clear as he moves toward the chair next to me. He is sitting as he speaks.

"Mind if I sit over here beside you? Got some questions of you, and I don't like yelling over the noise of the kitchen right here in front of us."

I nod my head yes, instead of speaking, for I am enjoying the piece of bacon that I am putting in my mouth. Oh, goodness, does it taste delicious? Oh yes, it does!

He extends his hand out, and I reach out and we shake hands.

"My name is Clint, and I'm a local from here and we were all wondering what happened up there on the mountain yesterday. Been a lot of activity down at the sheriff's office and over at the hospital, and none of those darn deputies will speak a word about what was going on. Are you one of those that they brought down from the mountain yesterday?"

I look at Clint and pause to gather my thoughts and swallow a bite of the biscuit and butter that I had put in my mouth while Clint was speaking. I know it is rude to eat while someone is speaking to me, but hunger and the sweet taste of the meal before me chases my manners out the door.

"Clint, my name is Glen." I extend my hand out and we shake hands one more time.

"Clint, I don't want to seem rude," I say. "But if the deputies aren't talking to the locals about what happened up on the mountain, then out of respect for the sheriff and the deputies, perhaps I shouldn't either."

Clint pauses.

"You're right, Glen, and it was rude of me to ask. But at least now I know you are one of those they brought down. Excuse my rudeness, and go ahead and enjoy your meal."

Clint begins to move away and I place my hand on his shoulder and ask him to remain seated.

"Clint?" I ask. "Your county sheriff and her deputies certainly impressed me yesterday. Is there anything you can tell me about her?"

His eyes light up!

"Oh, I see her now and then. I can tell you that she knows all the county folk by first name, and there is not a one of them who doesn't love and respect her. And the same goes for those deputies of hers. Every last man and woman of that department absolutely admires and respects her. 'Guarantee they would all lay down their lives for her if called on do so, and she would do the same for them. If there is any criticism of her, it would be that she spends a lot of county money sending her deputies and staff to training and different law enforcement seminars around the state, and to other states as well."

"Well, Clint, based on my experiences with her and her deputies yesterday, I would say that it is money well spent." As I speak these words, I look down at the end of the counter. The waitress and other men at the counter all have wry grins on their faces.

Just then, a booming voice calls out from the kitchen behind the counter. It is the cook, and he calls out loud enough for all to hear. At the same time, we hear the heavy front doors of the hotel close.

"Clint!" booms out the cook, "You better be careful 'cause the sheriff is in town!"

Clint's face lights up even more, and there is a new sparkle in his eyes as we both turn around and see the sheriff entering the cafe's swinging gate.

The sheriff pauses for a moment, looks at me, and then at the man beside me.

"Uncle Clint, Are you harassing my witness?" she speaks directly to him!

"Lily!" Clint calls out to her. "It is so good to see you today!"

"What is with this today thing, Uncle Clint? Uncle Clint, you see me every day. We share the same house. Remember?"

The laughter from the waitress and other customers is shaking the coffee cups lined up so neatly on the shelf behind the counter.

Lily! I like that name, and I can't help but join the others in their laughter. Was this Uncle Clint setting me up or what?

"Well, anyway, Uncle Clint. You move away from him because I've got to speak with him now, and we will be leaving as soon as he finishes his breakfast."

Clint moves over only one seat and Lily, the sheriff, sits down between us. Only one or two bites left on my plate, but I am not going to let them go to waste.

Coffee is set before the sheriff and she sips at it. She drinks it black. Me? I've got to have a little Sweet 'n Low and a bit of cream in it.

"Uncle Clint." The sheriff's voice softens, "when you go home, would you put Sawdust and Cat's food bowl out on the porch for them? I put their food in the bowl but was in such a hurry that I forgot to put it on the porch before I left."

"Already done so, and by the way, Sawdust and Cat say to tell you that they forgive you."

"Good. I wouldn't want those two to be upset with me." The sheriff replies.

The sheriff and I get up to leave, and Uncle Clint calls out to me as we are leaving.

"Maybe we can share a cup of coffee tomorrow morning, Glen."

"It's a sure thing, Uncle Clint." I respond.

"UNCLE CLINT!" scolds Lily.

"Don't worry, dear, I won't bother him if doesn't want me to," calls out Uncle Clint.

"You better not. Or you won't have any supper cooked for you for a week!"

And with those words, the sheriff and I leave the building.

THE MOUNTAIN

As we were exiting the cafe, the sheriff glanced at a man dressed in casual clothes and gave him a nod of the head. The man nodded back. Yep! He was a clone alright. One of my 24/7 guardians.

Once we were out on the streets, the sheriff begins to apologize for her Uncle Clint's teasing of me and not letting me know that he was her uncle.

"He can be such a tease sometimes, and he embarrasses me to no end, much to my aggravation. But he is such a dear man, and I know he loves me dearly as I do him."

"Oh please," I beg. "He is a delightful man, and he is surprisingly fit and moves with the grace of a 20—year-old, which is good for a man in his late 60s or early 70s."

"Good grief! Did he tell you that he was that age? The man is 85, for goodness sake!"

I am taken back! Usually I am pretty good at guessing someone's age; but boy, did I miss the mark on this one!

"No, no," I reply. "That was a guess on my part, and well, I was certainly wrong. Wasn't I?"

"You are not the first to guess his age wrong. He is as fit and spry as a mountain cat and will be that way for sometime. He has a lifetime of working in the saw mills, and all that can do is destroy you or make you stronger. He chose the stronger route." The words spoken by the sheriff about her uncle are words of admiration.

"But enough about my uncle," she says. "You have some work to do for us on the mountain, and that is where we are headed now." The sheriff reaches into the back seat of the SUV that we just entered.

She hands me a coat and speaks, "Put this on. It is going to be cold where we are going." And we head out towards the site where the helicopter dropped me off yesterday.

We are lifting off and all I can do is close my eyes and beg my memory not to take me back to South Viet Nam. Once you land in a hot LZ, you can never hear or see a helicopter without recalling that experience, much less ride in one! Your eyes can cloud out the scenery beneath you and replace it with the jungle and rice paddies you so often looked down on in the Nam!

At last! We are beginning our descent. There are persons already on the ground. Three or four others had joined us in the chopper; but, although I had been introduced to them, I was so intent on blocking out my memories I have no idea as to what their names or duties are. We are about to touch down near the same spot as the one that the chopper of yesterday also landed. Thank goodness, this is not a hot LZ!

We dismount and head up the boulder strewn terrain towards the crime scene.

It seems further away than it did yesterday.

Two deputies, who were already on the scene, stand and welcome us. It is obvious from their additional gear and clothing that they had spent the night on the mountain. I would assume they were protecting the crime scene.

Oh, my, I have just realized! I did not ask the sheriff how the professor was doing! A rush of selfish guilt washes over me.

We approach the deputies and the appropriate hellos and greetings are exchanged.

Small yellow flags on stiff wire are stuck in the ground all about us. Obviously, investigators have surveyed the scene and made a careful search of the area. Could I have expected less from this law enforcement team? I think not.

The sheriff now turns to me and says, "Mr. Becker. We would like for you to first take a look at your camp site, see if any of your gear is missing and then walk us through exactly what happened up here. Then we will gather all that has been left here and take it to our forensics team. Our forensics team was here yesterday and has already taken a few items down to the crime lab, but they need to take a look at the remaining items up here. The others who came up with us this morning are also on our forensics team. They will follow you and Detective Forman. All may have questions to ask you. Do you understand?"

"Yes Sheriff," I respond as I am led down toward my old campsite.

As I look at my campsite, the tent has been torn down, my gear scattered all about, and my backpack has been opened, everything in it scattered all about!

Detective Forman sees my startled reaction and says, "Mr. Becker, someone or something went through your gear before we got back up here yesterday and we would like to know what, if anything is missing."

I look at him, nod my head yes and begin to inventory my gear.

"Detective," I soon call out. "All that seems to missing is some of my clothing, a pair of river sandals that I used to ford streams with, and some of the canned foods that I have left." But I had lied a little bit!

Obviously, the trio of torturers had rounded back, went through my gear and took what they needed. They probably used my clothing to wrap their feet. Oh yeah, it would be Thor who now wears my river sandals. I can replace those items, but the one thing they took that infuriates me is my personal journal. Damn them! Not only do they know my name, address, and phone number, but also my personal thoughts. I had written my journal only for my children and their children so that they may one day look into the life and thoughts of their dad and granddad. My privacy and personal thoughts have been invaded! And I am livid with anger!

And my prescription medicines! The bottles are scattered all over, but I gather them up. And, yes, I need to start taking them right now.

But just as I am about to open and put them in my mouth, Detective Forman screams out with a voice that cracks the Sierra silence and echoes off its granite peaks!!

"Put the pills down, Mr. Becker! Do not put them in your mouth!"

I immediately pull the pills down from my mouth! They fall to the ground and I stare down on them!

"Leave all evidence as you found it, Mr. Becker!"

Ok, but why such an urgent demand to put the pills down? There was more than just concern over securing evidence in Detective Forman's scream at me to put them down!

More is happening here than I know about, and I move out of the area of my campsite.

What about my failure to tell the detective about the missing journal?

Why did I not tell this to the detective?

I will have to think about this for a while. I have got to take some time to calm down.

We all look up at the granite stone above, and the sheriff is looking down upon us.

"Mr. Becker, would you please now walk us through the events that happened?"

And I do so.

As I finish the tale of events, the sheriff says to me, "Mr. Becker, I am hoping that being here has caused you to remember any event, any action, and any words that you have failed to recall that might be awakened by your presence here. Do you recall anything that you have not previously recalled?"

I pause, and at the suggestion of her words, Yes!

"Sheriff, I recall Thor demanding the professor to 'Show me the signs! Show me the signs!' He said that over and over again!"

"Any idea as to what that meant, Mr. Becker?" asks the sheriff.

"No clue, Sheriff," I say.

The sheriff looks down on me and for whatever cause, I sense that she realizes I am withholding something. Something about her professionalism and insight into me causes that cause me to be uncomfortable about not disclosing that the fact that my journal was taken by the trio of torturers.

Perhaps it is just my personal anger towards the murderous trio that causes me to think such things.

But, no, this sheriff has that gift of discernment that can look into my eyes and sense that I have not been entirely forthcoming with her. With that thought, I know that I will have to tell her. But I well tell her in private.

After a thorough walk through of the events that happened to me, I am hammered by endless questions from the detective and forensics team. After their exhaustive and repetitive questions, the sheriff tells them to gather up the evidence and wait for another chopper to come pick them up. Then the sheriff, detective and I walk down the boulders to the waiting chopper. As it begins to start up, once again, I beg my memory to block out old thoughts of the Nam.

As we load up, I wonder. Where is Detective Jake Humphries? Shouldn't he be here?

We are headed down the mountain.

We are finally landing.

"Oh, thank goodness!" I mutter to myself.

We touch down, exit the chopper and the sheriff motions me to follow her to the SUV. Detective Forman heads for a waiting squad car that has blue and red lights flashing.

They leave. Hurriedly. But to where, I do not know.

As the sheriff and I buckle up in her SUV, she speaks out.

"Mr. Becker, I am taking you to the hospital. There, you will tell the physicians about your medical concerns and about any prescription medicine that you will need over the next few days. We need you to stay with us, for it is going to take a while for our forensic team to analyze all that we have gathered. Is that going to create any problems for you?"

I pause and think for a few moments and reply.

"Sheriff," I respond. "I am retired and, thank goodness that time is one thing I have plenty of." And then I silently think about my home, and my garden, and my roses.

Oh, my goodness, how selfish I am as I worry about the heat in the valley being so cruel to all I own there. The old professor is struggling so hard for his life, and here I am worrying about my small home and garden. I suddenly feel like a very bad person. But I care for my few small possessions and adhere to a very strict watering schedule. Never do I stay away for more than a couple of days, and roses are proud plants and are shamed by wilted petals. Almost every day, I follow the rule of five leaves and prune them regularly. But, at my roses' risk, I agree to stay for a few days.

Back to the moment, the sheriff is speaking to me. My selfish concern about my garden has blocked out some of her words. She continues, and then I rudely interrupt her and say, "Sheriff, there is a lot going on that I have no knowledge of. And I am concerned and confused. Is there anything that you can tell me that might clear up my state of confusion? I am trying to cooperate with you and your people, but there is a lot that is not being told to me. I have no idea as to what questions I should ask of you."

The sheriff pauses, momentarily glances over at me, continues to drive a short distance, and then pulls over to the side of the road and parks. She stares out ahead for a few moments and then begins to speak.

Her words have a chilling and frightening effect on my senses!!

"Mr. Becker, you are a fortunate man to be alive on this day. The men that you encountered yesterday are wanted by Interpol, the FBI, Scotland Yard, and almost all other international law enforcement agencies around the world. As I speak to you, there are agencies gathering in this county that may end up taking this case from me. But, for the moment, this county has jurisdiction over this case, and we intend to pursue it at due, but cautious speed."

Lily, the sheriff, continues.

"Your burning of their boots is going to be of great assistance to us. Their blood from their feet left on the granite rocks, as they came back to the scene, will probably confirm their identification along with the prints left on the weapons that you and the jumper so wisely brought down from the mountain with you."

I am sitting back in my seat, stunned at her words!

She continues.

"It will take a day or so to confirm the DNA that we have gathered, but again, we know who they are, and you and the professor are lucky to be alive."

"The men you encountered are wanted for several homicides and their methods of executions have ranged from strangulations, beatings, knives, guns and, yes, Mr. Becker, poisonings!"

There is a choking effect in my throat as I suddenly recall the screaming of Detective Forman to drop the pills from my mouth!

All of this is way over my head and difficult to comprehend. My concern about being involved in something I did not understand is only magnified as Lily continues.

"Mr. Becker, much has been discovered in the past 24 hours, and it is all difficult to condense into a short story. But please, be patient and I will try."

Lily speaks on, "And there is the man who you call Lucas."

"His name is Lucas Montgomery. He has been a thug and criminal since the age of 12. He has been arrested and convicted on many charges, ranging from shoplifting to manslaughter. The manslaughter charge he was convicted of was reduced from first degree murder to manslaughter because prosecutors were concerned that they could not prove all the elements of a murder charge. Right now, he has warrants out for his arrest for numerous charges of burglary, grand theft, assault and battery and two murders. We can only guess how many other crimes he has been involved in."

"The mouse-faced man that you described is only slightly more docile. He actually worked under the professor as a graduate student at UC Berkeley, as a research assistant. He is somewhat of a computer genius and could not help himself from hacking into confidential files of the university and helping himself to personal and sensitive data while working for the professor. And, yes, he hacked into the personal files of the professor.

When the professor discovered all of this, he turned the hacker, known as Felix Anderson, into campus police. Ultimately, Felix was dismissed from the university graduate program. The university attempted to keep all of this quiet, but the local authorities pursued the case. Although Felix was only convicted of lesser charges than they originally pursued, he was placed on probation and all chances of his continuing a graduate program at any other university were destroyed. As a result, Felix swore revenge on the professor. He disappeared for some time, until now."

"And the man you refer to as Thor is Thor Erricksen."

"At one time, he was a professor of anthropology at the University of Norway at Oslo. At one time, he was a respected authority in his field of study. But, for reasons unknown, he went rogue and began to obtain, steal and collect ancient artifacts, art and jewelry. And he went to any extreme to get them. The criminal charges against him include theft, blackmail, assault and battery, kidnappings and even murder. And, once again, that includes homicide by poisonings. Two guards in France were killed when they took their lunch break and ate their sack lunches. How the cyanide got in is not exactly clear, but Thor does not seem to mind leaving a clear trail of prints and other evidence behind him. In fact, he occasionally sends notes to the different law enforcement agencies, taunting them and citing facts that only the perpetrator would know. He appears to revel in his teasing and taunting of investigators."

"And Mr. Becker, he has sent us a note, telling us that you and the professor are dead men!"

I am frozen at these words of the sheriff. Not by fear, but by rage! To be threatened in this way is absolutely unacceptable! I feel as though I am caught in the kill zone of an ambush, and the only way that I know to respond is to attack and pull the attacker up close! Nothing is worse than living under threat of harm and intrusion! Now the combination of knowing that Thor has my personal journey and has invaded my most personal thoughts and has threatened my life has caused my only thought at this moment to be rage! I cannot conceal my feelings from this sheriff!

"Hold on, Mr. Becker!" This sheriff's gift is amazing!

"You are not going to do anything foolish! You, Mr. Becker, are going to remain in our protective custody and are to stand down and let this department do its job." The admonishment of the sheriff is stern and assuring, but my anger is only lowered a few degrees.

"Now, Mr. Becker, there is more to tell you, so may I go on? Are you in control of yourself so as to understand my words?"

"Yes, Sheriff. But could you please address me as Glen? Mr. Becker makes me seem so old."

The sheriff pauses, and then responds. "Not for the moment, Mr. Becker. And I only call you that out of respect."

I nod my head in approval.

She goes on.

"The professor is acknowledged by his associates, employer and students as being an excellent professor of history, and we have made an exhaustive investigation over the past day trying to understand what the perpetrators wanted of him. But insofar as his work at the university is concerned, at this time, we have not discovered anything that could expose him to the criminal acts that this terrible trio committed on him. And the professor has not told us all he can, I am sure."

I do not doubt her words about the professor not being as revealing as he could be. But I sense that he has good cause.

"However, the professor has personal interests, and I guess you could call them hobbies, that cause him to be so interested in California history he could be exposed to criticism by the university, and his associates. In other words, Mr. Becker, he almost borders on being called a treasure hunter.

The sheriff's statement stiffens my back, for my mind immediately recalls her words that Thor was a thief of ancient artifacts, art and jewelry! What could Thor have wanted from the professor?

The story continues.

"Now this really becomes almost laughable, Mr. Becker, but the professor over the past years seems to have become obsessed with his research of Sir Francis Drake of England and especially interested in

Drake's voyage up the California coast in the sixteenth century. And the professor was especially interested in Drake's fabled journey into what then was not named, but is now known as San Francisco Bay."

My thoughts recall that there are other bays in California named after Drake, and there are schools and even that grand old hotel in San Francisco, The Drake Hotel. However, as far as my memory goes, Drake's entry into the bay is conjecture and fable at best. But I recall that many have searched for imagined treasure buried by Drake in the bay areas, and no one has ever found any trace of it. But an interesting story, for I recall that Drake was known as a privateer who took great delight in raiding Spanish galleons for their gold and silver and proudly presenting his booty to Queen Elizabeth of England! 'Sometimes loading the Golden Hind and his other ships with so much booty that they occasionally made land and buried the treasures with the intent of returning or sending other ships to recover it!

The sheriff goes on, this time with what I sense to be some impatience on her part.

"Detective Jake Humphries is at UC Berkeley at this moment trying to serve a search warrant on the university so that we may look into the professor's office and files. But the university has had its staff, of what must be a hundred attorneys, file a motion opposing the search warrant and has created a legal hairball that our small staff at our county's DA office will take some time to untangle. We also are attempting to search the professor's home, but that has been blocked by the university's motion by alleging that anything related to the university that is in his home is subject to the same motion. Our search of the professor's home has been cursory at best."

"We were," she continues, "to request early on that the Berkeley police take a look at the professor's home. They found that there had been an unlawful break-in to the home and that things had been turned upside down. So, now, we believe we know the original site of the kidnapping of the professor."

"But, for now, we wait and try to do as much we can on this site and with you and the professor."

"Now, Mr. Becker," the sheriff questions me. "Do you have any questions, or is there anything you might like to tell me?"

"Yes!" Her question confirms my thoughts that she knew I was not telling everything about our trip up to the mountain and I am quick to respond!

"Sheriff, they took my personal journal!" and I hurriedly tell her about my name and other personal information in it. I try to explain about my anger stopping me from telling her sooner; and then, she interrupts me.

"'Don't need to apologize, Mr. Becker." "I would be offended too, but don't withhold any other thing from us again. Is that understood Mr. Becker?"

"Yes, Sheriff," I meekly respond.

"Do not worry about your home," Mr. Becker. "We have already contacted your local sheriff's department. The sheriff has extended full cooperation to us. He has sent deputies out to your home, and it does not appear that there has been any intrusion at this time. The sheriffs briefly spoke to some of your neighbors, and there does not appear to have been any unusual activity around your home. And, in fact, we have requested a 24—hour stake-out at your home, all at this county's expense, in hopes that Thor and his cohorts in crime show up there and an uneventful arrest can be made.

Could I expect anything less from this sheriff and her deputies? I think not.

They are so far ahead of me in this situation that I believe Thor may have committed a crime in the wrong jurisdiction this time. He may have, in the past, teased and tormented other agencies, but this little county's enforcement team may very well be his undoing!

So much has happened, and so much has been done by this team in so little time, that my head is spinning!

"Now, Mr. Becker," the sheriff continues, "We are having difficulty in finding the motive for the kidnapping and torture committed on the professor. Obviously, the dismissal of Felix Anderson from the university's graduate program plays toward a motive, but it can't be the cause of Thor's involvement in this crime. Something more has to exist that would bring Thor into this scene."

"Up on the mountain, you told us that you recall Thor calling out to the professor to show him the signs. Now that you have had some time to think about it, do you have any idea as what he meant?"

I quickly respond. "I'm sorry, Sheriff. I don't. I just simply don't."

"That's okay, Mr. Becker. Right now, we had better get you to the hospital and get your medications for you. The sheriff sounds genuinely concerned about my need of medications.

THE PROFESSOR

The sheriff starts up the SUV and drives out toward town and the hospital. She is silent for the moment, and my mind attempts to catch up on the events in the past day and a-half. Oh, geez!! Everything is happening so rapidly and in such sudden sequence that I have difficulty in recapturing all of it!

I have attempted to live a quiet and uninterrupted life over these past few years of retirement. Clinging to my privacy has almost caused me to become a recluse. I attend my grandchildren's school and other activities they are involved in; but generally, I keep to myself and avoid large groups of people. The exception is my daughter's occasional neighborhood dinners on holidays, such as the Fourth of July, Memorial Day, Labor Day or other holidays that her neighborhood celebrates. But, even then, I show up, eat the good food and soon excuse myself. Selfish, I know, but solitude, over the past few years, has become my best friend and she helps me to retain my sanity.

And now, here I am, trapped in a small Sierra town, a victim of becoming involved in an event that has overwhelmed me and has thrown me into a scenario filled with law enforcement personnel, an innocent professor, and a band of criminals. Oh, how I wish for my best friend, Solitude, to rejoin me.

The sheriff pulls into the backside of the hospital and pulls into a spot set side for law enforcement vehicles. There are several squad cars in the parking lot, and a few deputies are going into a back entry of the hospital.

The sheriff and I get out and we walk into the emergency room doors. The sheriff motions for me to have a chair in the waiting room and then says, "Mr. Becker, a physician will be with you in a while. He will want to know your medical history, and he'll want a list of medications that you are taking. Please be patient, for there are several people ahead of you. A deputy will be here shortly and I am going to leave you with him while I go upstairs and check in on the status of Professor Shumway. Excuse me please." And with that she starts to leave.

But before she does so, the receptionist calls her over to her desk and hands the phone to her.

The sheriff listens intently and seems to ask a few questions, hangs up the phone, then returns to speak to me.

"There has been a change of plans, Mr. Becker. There has been an incident that occurred just as we arrived here and I want you to come with me."

I can't help but ask, "What was the nature of the incident?"

She replies, "A deputy, who was monitoring the security cameras, spotted two men entering the hospital who matched the description of Thor and Lucas. There was an immediate response by deputies who were already in the hospital, but Thor and Lucas were seen on the security camera exiting a side door of the hospital. It appears that they have quickly disappeared. We are fairly sure that they are not in the hospital, but deputies are searching the building and grounds to be sure."

Oh, my! Thor is certainly bold and daring to have attempted to enter this building with so many squad cars outside. Or is he more stupid than bold! In either case, it appears that he is desperate to either finish off the professor or see if he can force the professor to "show him the signs!"

"But, for right now, Mr. Becker, Professor Shumway is conscious and is demanding that he speak to you and to you alone. Any idea what he wants to speak to you about?"

"Sheriff," I respond, "I know that I am saying this way too often, but I have no idea what is going on here or what the professor wants to speak to me about."

"Okay, Mr. Becker, let's go and see what he wants."

We walk down a hallway, enter an elevator, and begin to go up towards the professor's room.

We exit the elevator, turn to our right, we look down the hallway, and the scene in the hall way stops me in my tracks.

"Everything all right Mr. Becker?" asks the sheriff.

"Not really, Sheriff. Who are all these people in the hallway?" I ask.

"Most are Professor Shumway's family members. They starting arriving here last night and more are coming. Apparently, he has a lot of family members who care very much for him. We should all be so fortunate."

We approach the large group. There are both young and old, from infants in the arms of who appear to be their mothers, to elderly couples who seem to be comforting each other as they hold hands and watch our approach.

A young mother clutching her infant to her chest steps towards us and looks at the sheriff and asks, "Is this him? Sheriff Huntsmen, is this the man that saved my grandfather's life?"

The sheriff responds with a simple yes.

The question startles me!

What have these good people been told? And who told them? I cannot accept their belief that I had saved the professor, for, at this moment, all I can remember is that I cowered behind the granite far too long. If I would have responded sooner, the professor's injuries would not have been so severe. A coward does not deserve these kind people's gratitude.

No! No! This is not acceptable, and I cannot stand here and accept this family's gracious gratitude. I want to tell them to extend their kind appreciations to the smoke jumper who worked so feverishly over the professor on our trip down the mountain. Or to the paramedics who were there when we landed and began to immediately render aid. Or to the fine physicians and staff of this good hospital who have obviously done everything to save the life of the professor. But, not me. Oh, please, God, not to me! My emotions choke my throat, and I cannot speak.

But, one by one, they approach me and tearfully extend to me their gratitude. All I can do is stand still, my mind and mouth stunned into silence.

The sheriff senses my discomfort and politely excuses us. We walk up to the door of Professor Shumway's room. Two deputies stand by the door and remind me of great stone sphinxes guarding the entry way to an ancient pharaoh's tomb.

We enter.

The room is dimly lit, and a nurse stands over the professor, apparently checking his vital signs and the monitors that the professor is hooked up to. A deputy stands in the corner. A physician stands at the foot of the bed with what appears to be a chart on a clipboard. The physician notices our entry and walks up to us.

He speaks. He seems to know what we would like to ask.

"It is too soon to tell you that Professor Shumway is going to survive his injuries and heart attack, but at this time he is doing as well as we can expect. We are hopeful that if his recovery continues to go as well as it has, then he has a decent chance of survival. Right now, he is fragile, and all I ask of you is that you keep your visit with him to a minimum. We will be carefully watching his monitors during your visit. If they indicate undue stress, we will interrupt you and ask you to leave. Do you have any questions?"

The sheriff responds with a simple, "No, thank you, Doctor Williams."

The physician and nurse leave the room.

"Thank you, Nancy," The sheriff says to the nurse as she passes. Uncle Clint was right. This sheriff seems to know all of her county's citizens by name.

We stand side by side and approach Professor Shumway. His eyes flutter open and gaze out at us.

'Mr. Becker?" The professor's weak voice asks.

"Yes, Professor Shumway." I respond.

"Step closer, Mr. Becker so that I may see you better," he says.

"Yes, it is you, Mr. Becker," he says, "You are the chosen one."

The professor's words confuse me. I can see that they also confuse the sheriff as we exchange glances at one another, neither of us not understanding the meaning of such a strange greeting.

The sheriff excuses the deputy from the room, and she begins to leave the room, also.

I reach out and place my hand on her shoulder with a slight tug so as to let her know that I do not want her to leave. She looks down at my hand on her shoulder, and I immediately drop my hand to my side and speak out to the professor.

"Professor, I respect that you have stated that you wanted to speak to me and me alone, but I would like for Sheriff Townsend to stay and hear what you have to say. I trust her Professor Shumway and assure you that you can also trust her."

I anticipated resistance from the professor; but, instead, he looks and me and then begins to gaze intently into the face of Lily.

He speaks to her, extends out his weak hand to her and asks of her, "Please, come closer, my dear, and hold my hand."

His gaze is fixed upon her, and there seems to be a look of acceptance and trust that washes over his face.

"Yes," he says, "You are, my dear, the companion of Mr. Becker who has also been chosen. Please stay and hear my words."

These words are even stranger, but they seem to have a strength and conviction in them that both Lily and I sense. But we are still left curious and uncomfortable.

"Please, Mr. Becker, move over to the other side of my bed. Both of you stand closer to me so as to hear what I say to you. There is much to teach you and tell you about, and I ask for your patience in hearing all that I speak of."

I move to the other side of the bed, and in doing so, I realize that my sense of curiosity has reached a crescendo. I recognize the same exists in Lily.

"First," the professor speaks, "Please pay close attention to the signs that I am going to teach you. You must learn the signs, memorize them and never forget them, and you are to never reveal them to any mortal of this earth. That is, you are never to reveal them until called upon to do so by the Holy Prompter. Just as I have now been called upon by the Holy Prompter, to reveal them to you."

This conversation is getting stranger by the moment and is beginning to sound like the ranting of a religious nut. But the sincerity and conviction in the professor's voice lends credibility to his words. And the multitude of family members waiting outside in the hallway speak to the apparent credibility of this man's character and integrity so I am, more than just curiously interested in this man continuing to speak to us without interruption. And again, I sense the sheriff is, also.

And the signs that Thor spoke of. Are we about to learn what they are?

Professor Shumway demands of us that we watch his hands carefully, and he begins to place them on various parts of his body. Then he extends the palm of his hands upward, and they are seemingly prayerful. The movements of his hands and touching of his body continue, and he tells us to follow him in exact sequence. Both the sheriff and I fail in our initial attempts, but he patiently asks us to watch and follow him. We do re-enactments of his motions over and over again, both of us trying to recall and follow the lead of Professor Shumway. We are beginning to follow his lead, but he is insistent that we do it exactly as he shows us. The signs are confusing, in that they are so mixed and repetitive, but we both try to follow his direction. Eventually we are mimicking his lead in exact detail. The signs are beginning to cement into our memory.

Then, he asks us to show him the signs without his lead. We both fail. So we go over the signs again we are once again asked to demonstrate the signs without his lead. The sheriff succeeds. I fail.

So, once again, we follow his lead, over and over. He asks us to show the signs again. This time, both of us succeed. But that is not enough to satisfy the professor, and we are asked to demonstrate the signs over and over again. I can only hope that his monitors are not showing signs of undue stress, for I certainly feel stress in attempting to learn these signs.

After many demonstrations to show him that we have both learned and memorized the signs, Professor Shumway appears to relax a bit. The amazing thing is that both his body and voice has gained strength throughout this process while mine has weakened.

The professor has gained confidence that we both know the signs. He speaks to us. "Thank you, for being so patient in learning these signs."

What a gracious man, I think. Here he is, patiently waiting for us to learn these signs, in what may very well be his death bed, and he thanks us, for being patient.

He goes on. "And now I will tell you why these signs are so important by telling you a story of Sir Francis Drake that occurred on this continent many centuries ago. And I only ask of you to accept this story with an open mind and let the Holy Prompter tell you of its truthfulness."

Again, I ask myself, is this ranting of a religious nut? Or do I allow myself to hear this story to the end?

Again, the sheriff and I exchange glances, and both of us listen intently on.

"This is the story of Drake and his visit to the Bay," and the professor begins this tale.

DRAKE

I am only a cabin boy and aide to the captain of this great and wonderful ship, the *Golden Hind*.

The Golden Hind has earned the respect and trust of its crew, for she has carried them over mountains of high seas and uncharted waters that exposed her hull and crew to hidden rocks and reefs. She seems to sense and avoid those things that could rip her apart and throw all those aboard down to the dark depths of this beautiful, but frightening new ocean that most of this crew has never sailed before. Two other ships that began this dangerous voyage with us have already been lost, but the Hind's hull and sails are as tight and seaworthy as the day she began this trip. She responds quickly, yet smoothly, to the slightest touch of the wheel and her sails seem to catch the lightest of breezes and hurl her effortlessly over the whitecaps of this wondrous, but deceptive, ocean. She is one of those grand ships that seem to have a soul. She seems to enjoy this adventure and has sworn to keep all those aboard her safe. She is determined to reach the destination of this adventure with all hands alive. She is, to this crew, as a mother is to her children, as she wraps her arms around them and protects them from all things harmful.

And this crew feels the same about their captain. Drake! Captain Francis Drake!

Foremost, he is generous with his half share of all gold, silver and other booty that Queen Elizabeth allows him to keep. And his crew is always richly rewarded after Drake proudly, and boastfully I must say, presents the Queen with all that he has acquired for her. Drake delights in raiding Spanish galleons and their mule trains of gold and silver that are taken over the Spanish Main to waiting Spanish galleons off shore of the narrow neck of land between the new world's continents. He is ready for them as they transfer the treasures from the ships on one side of the continents to the other. Drake is one of the Queen's favorite naval officers, and she laughs openly at his humorous and boastful presentations of gold and silver. The members of the Queen's Court secretly hide their displeasure at her relationship with Drake, for after all, Drake is of common birth and should not have such a casual relationship with The Queen of England! But, as displeased as they are, they tolerate it. In stuffy silence.

Drake is somewhat of a scoundrel because I secretly believe that he reaps great joy in making both the Spaniards and the Queen's Court miserable. The royalty of Spain has placed a great reward for the head of Drake, and Drake takes great pride in knowing so.

His crew has great faith in his navigation skills, although they are somewhat unusual. Drake does not follow the text of most navigators. But nonetheless, he seems to carry this crew to whatever destination he seeks and arrives there in due time. And he enjoys a good laugh, along with good food and drinks. He doles out his share of rum with the crew and much of the formalities and separation of officers and crew are dispensed with. Yet, Drake maintains the appropriate dignity of his rank as captain, and his crew maintains their respect of him and his place as captain of the Golden Hind.

The Golden Hind are Drake are a good marriage, for they both have a sense of adventure but do not place their crew at risks not worth a good reward to all.

But now, there is a sense of tension among the crew as we sail northward along this northern most continent of the new world. The golden coast on our eastern side is breathtakingly beautiful, but its remarkable scenery does not dislodge the thoughts in our mind that Drake has not been himself since our anchorage on the narrow neck of land. I alone know what is on Drake's mind, and it is not comfortable knowing that Drake has not shared his experience with any of this crew, except for me. After all, I am only a cabin boy, and all I can do is listen, for I have no skills or experience that would lend any credible advice or assistance to our captain. The captain's trust in me to just sit and listen and not discuss any of the things that trouble him from time to time has been a humbling role in my relationship with him. He uses me, I think, to just sound out the things that concern him. Some of the things that he has told me in the past would have placed the crew in fear and may have caused disruption in carrying out their duties. Drake has shared most of his experience on the narrow neck of land with me, but the one thing he spoke of, but would not share with me, was the signs that he had learned while on the narrow neck of land. Drake admonishes me to speak of these things to no one, but to keep a written and secret accounting of these events. A prompting from an unknown source has told him to tell me these things, and Drake assures me that my writing of these events will one day have significance in ways that we cannot fathom. So, I keep a secret journal until Drake tells me to cease my secret writing of this adventure along the golden coast.

So now I am on deck, watching my captain look out over the ocean behind us. The crew has also noticed that Drake spends more time looking behind us rather than at his usual stance of watching forward as we sail north. This is unsettling to all of us.

Our anchorage by the narrow neck of land was only to go to shore and gather provisions of necessity. They were to include fresh water, native edible plants, fruit, and fresh game. Our stay there was only intended to be there long enough to gather what we needed, sun dry the plants, fruit, game, and then continue our journey. But the stay there became somewhat more eventful.

On our fifth day on the narrow neck of land, we came upon an unusual man; or rather, he came upon us. He was running through the forest, stumbling as he ran. It was apparent that the man was severely injured. When he saw us, he collapsed and we ran to his aide!

He was unusual, in that all we had seen on the land were local natives who avoided us but seemed to keep watchful eyes on our presence. This man had European features and was of fair complexion. But his language was not Spanish; and in fact, was different from any that the crew members had heard before. And this crew has experienced hearing many different languages, as they are experienced sailors and have traveled to many ports of the world. Drake ordered the crew to haul him to the Hind and have the ship's surgeon treat him. After finishing the day's toil of gathering much needed provisions, we returned to the ship. Drake asked me to join him in checking on the injured man.

We entered the surgeon's quarters. The surgeon looks at us, bows, shakes his head slowly, and leaves.

Drake sits by the injured man and looks at his injuries. The man looks up at Drake, and there is strength that seems to return to his face. The man holds out his hand to Drake, and says, in the Queen's English, "You are the one who has been chosen!"

The injured man appears to be as shocked by his words as Drake and I are!

But he is not shocked at his words as much as he is shocked by the language in which he spoke!

I have heard of people who suddenly begin to speak in languages that are completely unfamiliar to them, but they are only stories of superstition or fable. But something within me, that I do not understand, is prompting me to realize that I am witnessing this gift for the first time.

I see something in Drake's face that causes me to know that he is thinking the same thing.

The injured man looks at me and instructs me, "You are not to hear my words, but Drake will be prompted to tell you of those things that you will need to know. So, please now. Kindly leave us."

Drake motions me to leave the room. I do so.

I leave the room and go to prepare Drake's cabin for the evening. My mind is racing, and I am curious as to what the injured man has to say to Drake. But I will not ask Drake, for my captain will tell me only what he chooses to reveal.

After a great length of time, Drake enters his cabin, moves directly towards his desk and sits heavily in its chair. His face is long and drawn with fatigue, but there is a light about him that I have never witnessed before. Something has come over Drake other than exhaustion, and it is both enlightening and burdensome.

He sits at his desk with his back to me and reaches out for his quill and the ship's log. This is a daily routine for Drake to sit at evening's end and enter the events of the day into the log. He dips the quill into the ink, raises it and places it over the log. But he does not immediately begin to write. I excuse myself to the captain to go to the galley to get his evening meal, as I usually do. He says, "Do not be long, for we have much to discuss tonight."

I acknowledge his words and go to the galley.

When I return to the cabin, Drake is still sitting at his desk with quill over the log. But nothing has been written.

Drake has heard my entry into the cabin. After a few moments of pause, he turns to me and begins to speak.

"Sit with me and listen. And write."

Drake reaches for a new log and hands it to me. He tells me to get ink and a new quill. It is here that he tells me to keep a separate and secret log of the things he is about to tell me and a log of events that we are about to experience. I keep my tongue silent, but it is difficult to do so, for I am full of questions as to why I am to keep this secret writing secret?. He seems to understand my thoughts, for he tells me that there will be events of great significance that will be revealed later, that I cannot fathom now.

He speaks and I write.

"It is with great regret that I cannot tell you of sound reasons why I should believe the tale of the injured man who recently passed. However, there are promptings, unknown to me, that tell me what he spoke of is truth. Tomorrow we will go inland and gather the evidence I need to have to believe his words."

Drake continues with a long story. And I write.

The next morning, a scowl with a crew, Drake and I land ashore. Drake orders the crew to stay with the scowl and tells them that he and I will return before evenings fall. Together, Drake and I head out. Soon Drake pulls out a crude map from within his shirt.

It is truly crude and drawn with a faltering hand. The hand of a dying man.

We enter the dense vegetation and try to trace the path on the map and look for the landmarks so crudely drawn upon it. We sweat heavily as we advance into the dense and muggy forest and begin our trek. Amazingly, the landmarks appear, and we seem to be directed not only by the map, but by the promptings that both of us sense. Where do these promptings come from? Neither of us questions them, and we advance.

And sooner than either of us anticipated, we are at the site we seek. We begin to dig with the tools we had strapped to our backside. And there it is! The heavy satchel of leather that the dying man told Drake he would find!

We lift the heavy satchel out of its grave, heave its heavy weight upon the ground, and we both stare at it in amazement. So far, the truth has been told.

Drake reaches down and unfolds the leather satchel and pulls its sides down. And there before us, is a golden text with golden pages that gleam and glisten and glows in the tropical sun leaking down through the foliage above us! The dying man has been truthful in what he told Drake he would find!

Words are stamped onto the golden pages in a language that neither Drake nor I understand. But, if the words of the dying man are correct, they are a record of an ancient culture and people that lived upon the northern continent of the new world for many years. They are a testament that a Redeemer had appeared before them and promised them a glorious life after their mortal life that they could never comprehend. The dying man had told Drake that he was the last survivor of his race. A great war had taken place between his people and others on the great continent, and there were many who want to destroy this record of his people. He had pleaded with Drake to take this golden record with him and secure it in a place that was recorded on a map that accompanied the golden text. And the map was within the satchel.

Drake looked intently at the map, carefully folded it, unbuttoned his blouse and put it next to his body. He lifted the heavy satchel containing the heavy golden text, stood up—not without difficulty—and we began our return to the Golden Hind.

And now we are sailing north, towards a great bay on the golden shores that are on our eastern side.

THE BAY

On this day, Drake has been on deck since before the break of dawn. With map in hand, he stands in one place, and we all sense that we are about to reach our destination! The rising sun is casting sparkles upon the calm ocean. As we look eastward, it is blinding as it begins its rise into clear blue skies. The wind is light and to our advantage as we sail into an unknown and uncharted bay. And now, Drake steps toward the wheel and excuses the helmsman. Drake himself is going to take the Golden Hind through the opening in the coastline that we can now all see. All hands rush to the deck and look toward what we are all about to view for the very first time!

Drake orders men to the crow's nest to look out for hidden rocks and reefs. He sends men forward on the deck, so that they may look out and down so as to see anything that might tear our ship's strong hull. Drake orders the sails to half-mast, and we cautiously enter the channel that leads into the bay. Lines are being dropped, and crew is calling out the depths as the Hind glides slowly into the channel. There are great risks in this first entry that has never been attempted by any of the Queen's ships; or, as far is known, by any other ship of any nation of the old world. The Golden Hind responds smoothly with every slight turn of the wheel that Drake makes. She is as cautious as Drake is in finding her way through the channel.

And then the channel opens widely, and we look out on what truly is a great bay with blue waters, magnificent hills and scenery that line its shore. The bay is broad and long, and the water is smooth. There appears to be small islands made of rock scattered throughout. Drake looks at his map, and we begin to make what seems to be a slow and deliberate tour of the surrounding shores. Cautious sailors continue their vigilant search for rocks and reefs. The rock islands that we see in the bay heighten our concern, for who knows what other such islands might lie just barely hidden under shallow water. We all notice the heavy scarring of the shoreline that tell us the tides here are strong, with highs and lows that are extreme.

Drake is satisfied with his survey of the bay and positions the Hind in waters deep enough and far enough away from the eastern shore to avoid grounding at low tide. The sails are dropped, and the anchor hurls down from the Hind into the depths and finds ground to secure itself. The Hind slowly turns with the tide, and she is brought to rest. Her hull moans quietly, and she seems to settle down with a great sigh and begin a much deserved rest. She has served us well.

Drake orders all hands to stand down and rest and to tend to their personal gear. He orders a share of rum for all hands, and spirits are lifted. The tenseness that the men had felt is gone and they are now very much at ease. They see that their captain is pleased at our arrival at this marvelous bay, but they have no idea as to what now lies ahead of this adventure. The rum has a way of easing a sailor's concerns, and laughter is returning to the ship.

The captain returns to his cabin and begins to write in his log. I sit and write in my secret log.

THE LONG HAUL

It is a very busy morning. Drake has spent a great deal of time with the first mate, making arrangements for the captain's extended absence from the Hind. He will be taking part of the crew on this trek. Two scowls have been lowered, and men are bringing up provisions from below and dropping them into the scowls. Drake has ordered the first mate to select the strongest of the crew to man the heavy oars of the scowls. Strangely, he has ordered that they all bring heavy shoes. The men normally are bare-footed on the smooth and worn deck of the Hind. Heavy shoes are in short supply, but there are a few pair on board. The sail master has been ordered to make some from the leather we have available. A strange order this is. The first mate is ordered to keep all hands remaining on the Hind to be kept busy with cleaning and making any needed repairs. The last order is to keep the Hind safe and to have her ready for sail at a moment's notice. The first mate is told to be prepared for the captain to be gone for quite an extended time; and if for any reason, if it is compelling for them to escape the bay, to raise the anchor of the Hind and return when it is safe. They are to wait for our return. Drake cannot give the first mate any sense of time for our absence. We are going into unknown places, and we know not what difficulties we might face.

Finally, the scowls are loaded and manned. I stand in one, and Drake slides down the rope to stand beside me. The crew left behind on the Hind sends us off with salutes and wishes of luck, and we depart the sides of the mother of us all. The Golden Hind! Strong men on the haul on the heavy oars, and we begin our journey!

The last thing brought aboard the scowl was in the leather satchel on Drake's back. This is the first time the crew has seen the satchel. They have no idea as to what is in it but trust their captain to have need and purpose of it for this adventure. So, without question of their captain as to what is in the heavy satchel, and no questions as to where we are going or why, they continue to haul on the heavy oars steering in the direction the captain points.

We have found the mouth of the great river that leaks into the bay that the dying man had so descriptively given to Drake. The map confirms it. So does a prompting felt by both Drake and me. The crews of the scowls row us into the river, and a long journey of hard hauling against its currents begins. Just as the map indicates, it soon turns almost due north, and its waters are filled with great schools of fish. Its marshes are covered with so many numbers of waterfowl that I could not begin to count them. This is a rich land abundant with all that is needed to sustain mankind. The new world offers more than just gold and silver to all those who travel here.

After a few days of hauling heavy oars against this river's strong current, the crew's arms are weakening. Even Drake has given relief as he excuses the men from their oars and he takes their place as he lifts and hauls against the river. Foolishly, I have tried to haul on the oars, but I am much smaller than the strong men in the crew of this scowl, and my efforts are, at best, a hindrance, as I cannot match their pace. The feeble attempts of my skinny arms only arouse loud and boisterous laughter from the crew. The heavy hand of the man I tried to relieve comes to rest on my shoulder, and he relieves me of my oar. The laughter only rises as he sits in my place.

I can only aid the crew by scooping pails of water from the river and pouring water over their heads and bare-chested bodies to relieve them from the hot sun that bears down upon us. They laugh and sigh with each pail I pour.

We reach an eastern fork of the river. We turn into the eastern fork and continue on. At times along our journey, natives often see us and run along the banks beside us, laughing and following us along. They do not appear to carry any weapons with them, and they appear to be a happy people, more curious than concerned about us. In fact, on one occasion when we had to make shore and use ropes to haul our scowls through heavy currents, native children, men and women alike came and lifted the ropes to their shoulders and playfully helped us haul the heavy scowls against the current. Drake rewarded them with hardened lumps of sugar that he had brought along for his tea. Their reactions as sweetness washes over their tongues are of absolute delight to their faces.

After nonverbal acknowledgements of farewell, we re-entered the scowls and continued our long haul. I can only hope that the Spaniards or any other intruder to their land will not arrive, enslave them and force their Jesuit Priests upon them, for they are a happy and peaceful people that are truly blessed with a land of abundance.

We take another eastern fork of the river and set out upon it, but soon the current is too strong and the river too shallow for us to continue on in the scowls. Drake orders us to shore and we make camp. From here, we will continue on foot. We now see the purpose of the order of heavy shoes, for the shores of the river are of heavy stone and gravel.

That night, I write in my secret log.

The next morning one of the crews of the scowls is ordered to stay with the scowls and haul them up further into shore. Drake has noticed that this river has occasional high water, and he does not want them lost to a rising river. He orders them secured to heavy trees.

He then orders the other crew to put on heavy shoes and load up provisions on their back. Drake puts the heavy satchel, with the golden text inside, on his back and we begin our ascent up river. I plead with Drake to let one of the stronger men carry the heavy satchel, but Drake refuses. We begin our upward trek.

After a few days of an exhaustive trek, the river has narrowed to a simple small stream. There are great mountains all around us, and we are cooled by the shade of a great forest of towering trees. The high thin air is also cooler than the valley below us, but the trek is harrowing and difficult. The heavy shoes on my feet are uncomfortable. Blisters have formed and they bleed. Oh, how I miss my bare feet feeling the cool, moist, worn, and smooth deck of the Golden Hind!

We now see high peaks ahead of us that are crowned with granite and have patches of late summer snow still left in their shadows. We are surely close to the summit of these great mountains. Drake looks to his map and stops. He orders the crew to make camp. My captain drops to his knees and seems to be overwhelmed by the weight upon his back. He is exhausted from this long trek into this wondrous but difficult terrain. I approach him, and his quick look upwards at me surprises me. The look upon his face tells me that our journey is almost complete and that he is at peace. There is fatigue, yet relief, upon his face and I can only offer him assistance by removing the heavy satchel from his back and assisting him in rising from his knees. He walks up to each crew member, clasps their hands in a warm grip, and then stands backs and tells them to rest. He collapses under the shade of one of the great trees that surround us.

I prepare his meal for the evening. He awakens from his sleep, partakes of it, and then collapses in sleep once again. I write in my secret log, and then I, too, collapse in sleep.

Too soon, it is morning, and Drake has made what seems like a remarkable recovery from his physical state of the last eve.

I am feeling also extraordinary relief compared to last night's physical state. Something about looking upon the granite escarpments above lend Drake and me unanticipated energy. Our movements are quickened and hastened.

The crew is stirring in its morning awakenings, but not with the energy that Drake and I have.

Drake shakes the men from their sleep. He tells them to remain at this camp and that he and I will return in short time. We gather our things. Drake loads the golden text on his back and we move out. We head upward and toward the granite peaks above us. The crew puts up a sleepy protest about allowing their captain to leave their protection, but we depart and watch their fatigued attempts to fully awaken. We laugh out loud as we leave.

We are looking for a white pinnacle of rock that stands out in stark contrast to the dark gray granite of the peaks in front of us. Drake looks once again at the map, but we are guided more by promptings unknown to us than by the map. This experience is very much like our finding of the location of the golden text on the narrow neck of land. We do not understand these promptings, but we now place our faith in them. Suddenly, we leave the forest's edge and look out over the sea of granite boulders that have collapsed from the cliffs above us. And there is the white pinnacle of rock that stands out from all the dark granite behind it! Just as the dying man said it would be!

Drake turns to me, places his hand on my chest and tells me this is far as I am to go. My excitement is crushed.

But, I know that Drake has purpose in going forth alone. I disappointingly acknowledge his command and stand alone as Drake continues his ascent. I wait. I watch.

Drake steps behind the white pinnacle of rock and stands between it and the great granite cliffs behind it. I move to one side to witness what happens. Drake kneels and begins to display the signs that he spoke of but never revealed to me. I had seen him, in his cabin, rehearsing these signs, but was careful to avert my eyes for he said I was never to know them. I knew my captain had reason not to reveal them to me, and I never doubted his reason.

Suddenly, the wall of granite in front of Drake seems to be lifted, and a great opening appears in front of him. There is a soft glow of light that appears in the opening! I am shocked, so much so that I stumble backwards and fall! I lift myself on my elbows and look up at Drake as he enters what seems to be a great vault illuminated by a source that comes from within! Oh, my! There are events happening here that my mind cannot comprehend! Or even imagine! What am I witnessing?

I wait. And I wait. All of this has caused me to lose track of time, and I have no idea how much time has passed since my captain entered the great vault. It seems like hours, but the sun has hardly moved from the time Drake entered the granite vault.

And then Drake appears!

He steps forward out of the great vault, and the veil of granite that once hid it appears again. The vault is once again sealed.

He steps forward and begins his descent. He sees me and motions me forward. My feet are blistered and bleeding, but I leap hurriedly over the granite boulders between us and we greet each other. The leather satchel is empty of the great weight of the golden text, and there is a glow upon the face of my captain that I have never seen before. He reaches out and places his hand on my shoulders. He gazes at me and then says, "And now we go home. We go home to the Golden Hind!"

We bound down the rocks and into the forest.

We gather the men at our encampment and begin our descent to the scowls and men waiting below. The scowls are unleashed from the strong trees that secured them and placed into the river. The river is on our side, and the current is to our advantage this time. The crew hauls at the heavy oars as we seek the mouth of this great river that leaks into the bay. The natives who helped us haul the scowls up the current are back, to cheer us on as we pass them by. The hot sun that had beat down on us in our trip up the great river is cooled by a southwest breeze and light clouds that temper the heat. We enter the bay, and we see the Hind glistening in the sun! She seems to bounce on small white caps of water beneath her. Her dance is one welcoming us for our return. We approach and her crew is welcoming us forward to her side. I step onto to her smooth and worn deck with my tired and blistered feet, kneel down and kiss my sweet mother's deck.

On morning's rise, the Hind's anchor is drawn, her sails are unfurled at half mast, and we begin our exit from the great bay. She glides responsively to our captain's touch of the wheel and we pass through the narrow channel and head out to open sea.

Sails are raised to full staff, and we continue on our journey. A journey that will take us around the world!

I write no more in my secret log.

THE MOMENT!

The professor's voice stalls, and Lily and I are spellbound. I look at the sheriff and my mind is full of questions, but what do we ask? There is no logic to this story that we have been told. There is no reason to believe that it is true. However, there seems to be a reason that we should believe what this man is telling us. Where are these promptings of belief coming from? I do not know.

The professor speaks again.

"You are both chosen to receive the things that I give unto you. You are charged to safeguard and store them in the great vault that exists in a holy place." With those words, the professor calls for Nancy, the nurse, and asks that she bring, his grandson, Nathan, into his room.

Nathan enters the room. And on his backside is a heavy leather satchel! Nathan deposits the heavy leather satchel at his grandfather's bedside and excuses himself.

The professor reaches into the heavy leather satchel, pulls out a leather-bound and worn book. He extends to us a log! A simple book of a log that is of old bindings and fragile pages that look to have been exposed to many years of time's toll. The secret log of a cabin boy of century's past!

Lily and I look at the log. And with an approving nod, I agree to Lily's careful touching and turning of its fragile pages. The professor accepts our curiosity and approves our reading of the log. It is written in the old style of the Queen's English. We read, and I, on occasion, have to stop and ask Lily how she interprets some of the content. Its pages are fragile but Lily's tender touching of its pages, and of its content, is appropriate. The story that we read is consistent with the professor's tale and confirms all that he told.

The professor senses that his story is accepted by Lily and me and sighs with great relief!

And with the relief within him, the professor tells us, "My burden has been passed. And now, the Prompter tells me that I will enjoy many years with my family."

He continues, "Know that your burden will reward you with great happiness upon its completion and that years of happiness will follow upon its passing. Your life together will bear great joy and completeness that cannot be fathomed in mortal terms!"

And with those words, the professor excuses us and asks Nurse Nancy to allow his family to visit with him.

What a moment in his life!

The evening is late, and as the sheriff and I leave the professor's room, the great stone sphinxes at his door still stand guard over his room. I am exhausted from the day's event, and so is Lily. Exhaustion is apparent on both of us as we go down the elevator and back to the emergency room to get the prescriptions that I now certainly need. After a brief stop at a pharmacy, she drives me to my hotel. It has been a long day of investigative procedure. But before she drops me off at my hotel, I look down at the heavy leather satchel that contains the young cabin boy's log and begin to lift it so as to take it with me. The sheriff halts me and tells me to leave it on the seat.

"Sheriff," I exclaim!

"Mr. Becker," she says. "As sheriff of this county, I am to preserve all evidence that concerns a crime. I have no choice in this matter."

"But!" I begin to say. She stops me before further protest.

"I assure you, Mr. Becker that it will be well secured. All I have to do is tell the evidence clerk not to look at its pages and she will do exactly that. She is a good officer and will do as I say, for she is a woman of good integrity and I trust her."

As a result of her authority, I am forced to comply, but as she pulls away from the hotel, I am left with great concern.

Deputy Bentley is waiting on the sidewalk of the hotel. He escorts me in, and despite a harrowing day, my appetite is heavy. I soon retire to my room, shower, and return to the country cafe behind the swinging gates.

And such a wonderful menu that I am presented with!

I am not looking at the steak menu. No need to do so. There are selections that include:

Baked pork chops with green beans and red bell peppers accompanied with stuffing and turnip greens! Southern fried chicken and mashed potatoes and delightful side dishes of black-eyed peas or red beans! The latter would have been my choice if not for the following choices that include a no-so-appealing generic dish of noodles and red sauce that immediately turns my attention to a mushroom-laced dish of meatloaf, mashed potatoes and gravy, green beans with bacon strips and my favorite side dish, summer squash and red onions! I choose the summer squash and anticipate the serving.

These are foods of menu and recipes that used to feed the hungry appetites of the hardened men who worked long hours in the saw mills that once thrived here. The saw mills are long gone, but the meals and recipes that sustained them in a long day's work are still on this cafe's menu. I wallow in the delight of the great food that they serve. Who needs a steak menu?

I finish my evening meal, lean back in my chair, and think, "I will most definitely have to take a long walk in the morning to keep this caloric overload off my waistline."

THE MORNING

I awake with a start, once again, to the scent of bacon as it wafts upward to my room! But I am not as starved as I was yesterday morning, for the heavy evening meal that I enjoyed is still weighted in my body. My shower and shave is at a slower pace this morning and when done, I put on fresh clothes that the sheriff's department had left with Lizzy last night. The service of the sheriff's department and this hotel cannot be complained about. I deposit my clothes of yesterday in a sack left by Lizzy and hang them on the door as she had asked. It's nice to receive a little personal attention and service on occasion.

My walk down the stairs is at a slower pace, and I do not have to feign being patient as I open the swinging gate of the country cafe. Upon my entry, I am greeted with a loud, but friendly, voice.

"Good Morning, Glen!" It is Uncle Clint. He motions and calls me to sit with him at the cafe counter. I am most glad to do so and sit beside him.

"Lily told me that you and she had a busy day yesterday." But Uncle Clint does not ask me about the events of yesterday. I can only assume that he respects the fact that I will not speak about what happened, and Uncle Clint goes on and speaks of different matters.

Uncle Clint is a jovial man with a quiet laugh and continuous tongue that begins to speak of his experiences of long hours in the saw mills and about his now passed good wife, Hazel. Apparently, he has a history of a rich and warm life, earned by hard labor and devotion to his community and family. It would be difficult not to like this delightful old man. And I do like him, just as all who are here and those who enter the café so obviously do, as they all accept his warm greetings and return the same to him. His conservation with me is interrupted several times as people who enter and leave. All come to his side and wish him a good day. I do not mind such interruptions, for they only confirm that this man is of good character.

I order only coffee and biscuits and gravy. Even that small order seems heavy as I slowly eat my breakfast and listen to Uncle Clint. It is a good morning!

Uncle Clint finally excuses himself to go home to water and hoe his garden and to check on Sawdust and Cat. He says that he hopes to see me in the morning and exits towards the swinging gate. He gives warm waves and goodbyes to all those present. I hope that we see each other again in the morning.

As I finish my last cup of coffee, I get up and immediately feel the effects of overeating and wish to go on an extended walk. I walk towards the cafe doors and see my personal guardian looking at me, peeking over the top of a morning newspaper. I would like to wish him good morning, but know that I should not and walk out to the desk and ask the person behind the lobby desk if I could use the phone to call the sheriff. She hands the phone to me, and I make my call.

Madge answers the phone, and I ask, "Madge, this is Glen Becker down at the hotel and I desperately need a long walk this morning. Would you please ask the sheriff if I could go out for a walk?"

Madge answers back, "The sheriff is about to walk by me on her way to a briefing. Hold on a moment, Mr. Becker."

Madge soon speaks again.

"Mr. Becker. The sheriff asks that you be patient and she will soon send a deputy down to accompany you."

"Thank you, Madge." And I hand the phone back to the clerk.

So I step into the reading room of the lobby, pick up a newspaper, sit in one of the plush chairs, and wait.

Okay, so I am not incarcerated in a jail cell, but I still feel detained and uncomfortable about not leaving the hotel on my own. But at least my place of confinement is warm, comfortable, and has excellent food and service. All the same, I realize that freedom is a wonderful thing and the slightest feeling that I cannot come and do as I please, unsettles me.

I am almost finished reading every column and every word of the newspaper that had kept me from boredom of my long wait when I look up. Wouldn't you know? It is Deputy Bentley who has come to accompany me on my walk. I stand up after polite greetings and we walk out through the heavy hotel doors.

We begin our walk along the sidewalk that passes by stores with historic facades. Every thing is small and quaint. Bells ring as customers enter and exit through the door of the small stores. We eventually turn onto a street that soon leads us into a tree-shaded neighborhood of old, but solid, homes with carefully tended yards and white picket fences. Everything is well maintained and the scent of summer's flowers waft through the air. This is a most pleasant walk.

Deputy Bentley speaks first. "The sheriff is furious this morning," he says.

"Oh?" I respond.

"Yes," Deputy Bentley continues. We received another note this morning from Thor telling the sheriff her department is nothing but a bunch of country hicks and that if we continue to interfere with him, she and some of us will be added to his list of soon to be deceased. Now this whole damn matter has become personal for the sheriff and the rest of us. She has not wanted to alarm the community with all of this, but posters, along with notices on Internet sites, are being sent out to all hotels, cabs, restaurants, train stations, airports and every place else we can think of, in hopes that someone has seen those three jerks and we can finally apprehend them. We are even sending out deputies on horseback to all the possible campsites that they might be staying at. The sheriff is throwing every resource into this manhunt, and hopefully, we can put an end to this case very soon."

His words stop me in my tracks!

Who is this man, Thor? Who is he, who thinks he can intimidate these fine officers of the law and prevent them from doing their duty?

He knows this will only heighten their determination, and he must be enjoying the taunting of them. His ridiculous sense of teasing will be his undoing, I am sure.

I step forward with a quickened pace as my anger drives me forward.

I would speak more to Deputy Bentley, but my anger prevents my tongue from forming words that would be accepted as civil. So we continue on through this wonderful, small town.

We arrive back at the hotel, and Deputy Bentley says polite wishes of a good day to me and I extend the same back.

I enter and start to turn towards the stairs that go to my room when the clerk at the lobby desk calls out to me to approach her. I turn and walk toward her.

She tells me that a gentleman has asked me to join him for breakfast. I thank her and turn towards the country cafe. She halts me. She tells me that the gentleman is sitting in the formal dining room.

I enter the dining room, and there are two men sitting at a table in the dimly lit room. I approach them and am suddenly halted!

It is Thor! And seated beside him is Lucas!

Thor speaks to me and says, "Please, come and sit with us. Can we order you something to eat?"

I glance over my shoulder and look for my guardian!

I hesitate.

Thor's voice lowers but has a much more threatening tone.

"You sit, Mr. Becker, or your personal deputy will never see another day."

What have they done?!?

Where is Felix, the mouse?

I glance about again, approach the table, and sit. All my senses are on alert.

"Thank you, Mr. Becker," this horrid man says. Such politeness coming from an evil mouth disgusts me.

"Just wanted to chat with you this morning, Mr. Becker, and hopefully have a polite conversation. Our first meeting was quite disagreeable, and I hope that we might get along better after you hear what I have to offer you."

I sit in silence.

"Oh, by the way, your personal deputy is a little tied up for the moment in your room and cannot join us. But don't worry. Felix is keeping him company. And just so you know, Felix does not have the skills with a knife that you may have learned at Fort Bragg, but he enjoys using one when his victims are bound and secured."

A not-so-subtle threat! How does he know that I was once at Fort Bragg, North Carolina, while attending the special warfare school there?

Thor sees the question on my face and continues.

"Oh yes, Mr. Becker, I would like to thank for the insight you gave me about you and your life."

Thor reaches down and pulls up my personal journal and places it in front of me. I reach out, grab it and pull it to my chest.

Thor then says, "I am most happy to return it to you."

This man's forced politeness is only infuriating me!

"You are not being very polite, Mr. Becker, don't I at least get a thank you?" and Thor then quietly laughs.

This one-sided conversation continues.

"Mr. Becker, I have learned from your journal, that you are living a quiet and quaint, simple lifestyle. You live in a small home, have a fixed income, and do not get out very often except to take ridiculously long treks through the Sierras. You suffer from injuries that happened in Viet Nam and illness resulting from exposure to Agent Orange."

Thor laughs quietly again and speaks more.

"Oh, Mr. Becker, how could you not be upset with all that this warlike nation has done to you? I am going to offer you a chance to have what you deserve and live out your years with riches that will provide you with all that you want, travel where you want, live in a grand house, and never have to be concerned about not ordering any food you want, in any restaurant, in any country of this world. All you have to do is show me the signs that the professor showed you and we will both be rich beyond your wildest dreams!"

I sit in still angry silence with no thought in my mind of joining this evil band of criminals.

Thor responds to my silence.

"Oh, I see you need some time to think about it. Well Mr. Becker, you have until this time tomorrow. If you cannot see fit to show me the signs, then you and your pretty sheriff will have dues to pay, and I always collect from those who have what I want. We are going to leave you now. You will give Lucas and I time to leave, and time for Felix to come downstairs and leave with us. As soon as we all leave the hotel, you are free to do as you want."

What arrogant confidence this man has!

Thor reaches for his cell phone, places a call, and in moments, I see Felix coming into the dining room. Thor and Lucas stand and head down what appears to be a hallway that must lead to a rear exit of the hotel.

I rush towards the lobby and call out to the clerk to call the sheriff and tell her to send deputies to the hotel immediately! She hears me and sees the urgency for the call. I head for the staircase, and the phone is in her hand before I reach the top of the first flight of stairs!

I reach my room, tear open the door, and see the deputy bound on the bed by his own cuffs. Duct tape is over his mouth that could possibly suffocate him! I stand over him and see heavy bruises on his eyes and a gaping slash on his right side of his face that could have only been made by Felix's knife! What a cowardly and cruel man that Felix must be!

As I begin to remove the duct tape from the deputy's mouth, there are sirens of squad cars sounding outside! The sheriff's department has been called! And now there are thudding sounds of footsteps bounding up the creaking stairs towards my room! Thank God that aid is coming towards this injured deputy!

And in moments, the room is filled with deputies and first responders.

I stand with my back to a wall as the deputy is attended to.

All present are responsive and most attentive to the care and aid of the injured deputy. I stand in shock of this moment! All this has happened because of my involvement, and I am so sad for it all.

The paramedics are placing the injured deputy on a gurney. Then the sheriff enters the room. She first looks at her deputy and offers him words of concern and then looks to me.

"Mr. Becker, are you all right? Do you need medical attention?"

I respond with a trembling voice, "No, Sheriff, I am fine."

"No, Mr. Becker, you are not!" and orders two deputies to take me to the lobby and remain with me.

I stumble as I descend the stairs. If not for my grip on the handrail and the sudden clasp of a deputy on my shoulder, I would have tumbled to the bottom. My knees are weak at this moment of terror as I feel I am to blame for the horrible slashing of the good deputy's face.

Oh, how I wish for my simple and quaint lifestyle that Thor had so accurately described!

Why has my good friend, Solitude, abandoned me?!?

I sit in the reading room of the hotel with my own two great stone sphinxes that stand next to me.

The gurney is brought down the stairs and there is a flurry of activity of deputies going up and down the stairs.

Now I see Detective Humphries, who has returned from the bay area and is on his way up to my room.

Guests of the hotel are observing all this activity, and I am afraid that I am the cause of the disturbance that interrupts what should have been a most pleasant experience in their lives. I am sorry!

I wait. And I wait. And my two great stone sphinxes stand patiently by my side.

I notice what must be a forensic team enter the dining room and carefully photograph and bag the dishes and silverware from the table where Thor and Lucas had eaten their breakfast. Detective Humphries has come down the stairs and seems to be interviewing the frightened lobby clerk. He takes careful notes as he speaks to her.

Finally! The sheriff comes down the stairs, approaches Detective Humphries, exchanges a few words with him and they both approach me.

"Mr. Becker," the sheriff says. "I hope that you are okay now. Do you need anything?"

"No sheriff, I am okay, just a little shaken up; but really, I am fine." I hope my response is convincing.

"Well, Mr. Becker, we are going to ask you to come to the jail. Detective Humphries is going to need a step-by-step accounting from you concerning all that happened here this morning." She continues, "I thought about having you spend the day and night at the jail, but that would seem punitive and I do not want to put you through that. When you return to the hotel, Lizzy has agreed to place you in a different room because your room now is a crime scene. We are going to secure it for a while until the forensic team has completed its investigation of it. There are going to be uniformed deputies that stay with you tonight, as our attempt to have a civilian-clothed deputy watch over you has obviously failed and did not fool Thor."

"How is the deputy? Is he going to be alright?" I ask.

The sheriff answers, "He is going to be okay. There is going to be some surgery to close and later conceal that gaping slash on his face, but he is a strong man and will be back on duty in a short time. And every deputy in this county is now determined to bring this case to a close. You do not harm one of their own and walk away from this force unscathed!"

I believe her!

We exit the hotel.

NORMAN ROCKWELL, SAWDUST AND CAT

It has been a long day, complete with exhaustive repetition of the morn's events with Detective Humphries. Oh, how I long for once before uninterrupted life of peace and solitude. How did my best friend, Solitude, escape me?

Detective Humphries and I are finally interrupted by the sheriff.

She apologizes for the long time I have spent with the detective and tells me that I am to retire to my room. I am so glad!

I enter the creaking doors of the hotel and am guided by my two great stone sphinxes to my room.

The eve is falling, and although not dark yet, I enter my shower and let cool, then warm water, pour over my body! Oh, what relief! I shave and then seek the smooth and cool comfort of the sheets of my bed.

I sleep better than I anticipated and awake to morning's warm sun seeping through my room's curtain. It is late for me to wake up at this time. It has been an unexpected night of good sleep, and my appetite has returned as I head down the stairs for breakfast.

"Where the heck have you been this morning? says Uncle Clint as I enter the country cafe's swinging door.

"Sorry, Clint!" I exclaim. "I slept in a bit late this morning."

"Well, come on over and share a meal and coffee with me," says Uncle Clint.

I am glad to do so.

My appetite is strong this morning, but I remember the sheriff's admonishment and order the cafe's breakfast special, eggs and bacon with country potatoes. Oh, such a morning delight.

And Clint's good company only adds to this morning's enjoyment.

We sit together, and the same good interruptions that occurred yesterday happen this morning as people walk up, engage in brief conversation and wish Uncle Clint a good day! He returns the kindness, and our conversation continues. Or, at least his part of the conversation continues, as his persistent tongue goes on. He does not bore me.

Uncle Clint begins to excuse himself for the same reasons he used yesterday morning . . . to water his garden and check on Sawdust and Cat. But before he does, he extends an invitation to me.

"Lily told me this morning that she will have a short day today and to invite you to dinner this evening. I am going to draw you a map and I expect you to show up. Oh, let's say around seven, when the day's sun shadows are getting long."

Uncle Clint begins to sketch a map on a napkin, and I am surprised by such an invitation from Lily and Uncle Clint.

I respond the only way I can. "Uncle Clint! Is this appropriate?"

"If Lily asks, how much more appropriate could it be?" Uncle Clint answers.

"Well, I would love to come, but should I bring anything?" I ask.

"Bring only a good a sense of hunger. Lily is a great cook," says Uncle Clint.

"Okay. I look forward to dinner, Uncle Clint," I say.

"See you there!" and with those words, Uncle Clint leaves the cafe."

There has been little activity this fall day. I choose not to go on a walk, partly because my stomach does not feel as full as yesterday, but also because of my remembrances of yesterday. No one has called me or spoken to me about the current events of the ongoing investigation, and I am bored. I welcome the boredom, for I do not want anything to happen that is even close to equaling yesterday's events.

I have made vain attempts to suppress my excitement and hopeful anticipation of Lily's invitation to dinner this eve.

So, I wait and watch the clock and look at the map that Uncle Clint had drawn out on a cafe napkin.

I enter the reading room, look over the books on the bookshelves and, yep, both Hemingway and Twain are there. I decide to read a bit of Hemingway; and despite the great author that he is, he cannot stop my mind from anticipating dinner at Lily's tonight!

At last. It is close enough to seven o'clock that I should begin my walk to Lily's and Uncle Clint's. It is difficult to conceal my eagerness to go. I put Uncle Clint's crude map in my shirt pocket and approach the two deputies who have never been far from my side. I tell them of my invitation to Lily's home for dinner, and there is a startled look on both their faces.

One of them speaks. "Well, certainly, Mr. Becker, I will escort you there, but I am surprised at Lily's invitation. However, I can assure you that whatever she prepares for dinner, it will be great! We all know her kitchen and the great food that comes from it." It is Ben, who is to escort me to Lily's. The other deputy will remain in the hotel.

We begin our walk, and the late summer sun is casting long shadows of the cooling trees that line the streets. A most pleasing evening walk!

There is no need of any use of the map that Uncle Clint gave me, for Ben knows the direction towards the sheriff's home. But it is further than I had expected. I begin to hurry my pace, for I am concerned about the time and do not wish to be late. Ben assures me that we will be there soon.

And we are!

We approach a house that has been well cared for, with a steeply pitched roof that will ward off winter's deep snow. It is freshly painted and surrounded by summer's flowers. There is a peach tree on one side, and I secretly hope that I am offered one of its remaining fruits. A sweet, yellow peach sounds awfully good to me right now.

We walk up to the gate of the home's white picket fence and I notice Uncle Clint sitting on the front porch. He stands up to greet us. A somewhat large, yellow dog comes down from the porch. It appears to be a golden retriever mix, with perhaps some hound in it, for it has large and long floppy ears that appear to be misplaced on the wrong dog. But its approach is with an open mouth and wagging tail. A sure sign of a friendly dog. And a cat is walking with the dog that weaves in and out of the dog's every step as they approach. They must be Sawdust and Cat.

We are welcomed warmly by Uncle Clint, Sawdust, and Cat.

Ben is excused by Uncle Clint, but not without protest from Ben. Uncle Clint offers assurance that I will be safe in the home of the sheriff.

"No, now, don't you worry any, Ben. Glen could not be safer than here at the sheriff's house. She is in the kitchen right now, so you just go on back to the hotel. We will call you when Glen is ready to go back."

Ben hesitates and then leaves with a polite, but reluctant, good-bye.

Uncle Clint motions for me to follow him and says, "I've got sun tea brewing on the backyard table. We'll go get it and then go into the kitchen and see Lily."

We step off the walkway and onto grass that is a rich lush green. My feet seem to be stepping on crushed velvet. We walk around the side of the house and I see the garden that Uncle Clint seems to always use as his excuse to have to leave town and go home. The garden is well maintained and filled with all things wonderful to eat.

Sawdust follows alongside us and the well choreographed weaving between the legs of Sawdust that Cat performs goes on. They dance well together.

We round the corner of the house and step into the backyard. There is a woodshed in the very back, and an axe is driven into a chopping block where Uncle Clint must split their firewood for winter. The woodshed is filled with what already must be their winter supply. It takes busy hands to keep this house in such good shape, and even busier and stronger hands to gather, chop and store such a large amount of firewood. Uncle Clint is not an idle man in his retirement years.

Uncle Clint picks up the brewing sun tea and we step up onto the back porch. He enters the back door and steps into the kitchen. I stand for a few moments in the doorway and see Lily standing at the kitchen counter. She has a light blue gingham dress with small yellow flowers. She is wearing a white apron and has a pair of flats on her small feet. Her hair is tied up into a bun on the top back of her head.

This sudden transition of Lily from a professional and uniformed officer of the law into a beautiful and delicate-faced woman is amazingly wonderful!

Uncle Clint has moved to her side and she tells him to put the tea on the counter.

She has not yet noticed me.

I let the screen door close behind me and she turns her head towards me. There is a look of surprise on her face.

Her mouth is slightly puckered and is slightly open. She stands holding a serving tray and a large wooden spoon in her hands. Uncle Clint is looking over her shoulder at me and has a wide, wry smile on his face. One eye brow is lifted much higher than the other.

This is surely a Norman Rockwell moment in a country kitchen.

Lily's voice also has a sound of surprise in it!

"Mr. Becker! What are you doing here?"

I suddenly feel my face redden as embarrassment washes over me and the only thing my mouth can do is stammer words of apologies that even I cannot understand.

Uncle Clint is snickering and laughing, and he escapes into another room!

Lily seems to suddenly realize what has happened and calls out in a scolding voice!

"Uncle Clint, you get into this kitchen right now! And you apologize to Mr. Becker for what you did to him!"

Uncle Clint re-enters the kitchen but cannot suppress his snickering and laughing!

Lily scolds him again. "Uncle Clint, you have to stop trying to be a matchmaker for me and promise me that you are not going to do anything like this again!"

Lily's scolding of him is of no effect, and his giggles and laughter are now way out of control.

Uncle Clint's laughter is contagious and soon, I can't suppress myself from snickering and laughing out loud.

The stern look on Lily's face begins to soften, and the contagion strikes her. We are all laughing hard as tears flow from our eyes. Uncle Clint has survived his devious little scheme, and I am beginning to get over my embarrassment.

I gain control of myself, apologize to Lily and begin to leave. And Lily speaks out to me.

"Please, Mr. Becker, don't leave. You deserve a nice meal for what this evil uncle has done to you, and there is plenty for all of us. So please stay and enjoy it with us."

I quickly agree to her invitation. And Uncle Clint giggles a little more.

"It'll be a few minutes before I get the table set, Uncle Clint, so please take Mr. Becker into the front room or show him about the house, if he would like." Lily calls out.

Uncle Clint motions me to follow him and we go into their front room which is exactly as I thought it would be.

Solid and strong antique furnishings compliment the subtle and soft colored wall papering. There are family photos placed about the room, and on one end table is a photograph of Uncle Clint and a most attractive woman by his side. She must be Hazel, Uncle Clint's good wife he so proudly spoke of in our cafe conversations. He sees me looking at it and confirms my thoughts.

He takes me on a tour of their small home, and we go down a hallway that has more family photos hung on its walls. Wouldn't you know? On the wall at the end of hallway is a Norman Rockwell print hung in a heavy wooden frame that confirms my earlier Norman Rockwell moment in their country kitchen.

We enter a room that has a desk with a computer on it. There are file cabinets against the wall. And on the wall are awards and diplomas of graduation. I look closer at them and see that Lily has a Master's in education from Stanford University and a Juris Doctorate degree from its law school. It should not surprise me to see all this, but I am surprised at the dates on the degrees. Lily must be older than I had suspected. And I mention this to Uncle Clint.

"Oh yeah, Lily looks very young for her age. Always has." Uncle Clint responds.

"Well, that puts her less than ten years younger than me and I am surprised." I say.

"Both of you look young for your ages. You both must have good family genes," I continue.

"No." Uncle Clint answers. "It's because we have both lived most of our lives up here in the high country, and these big conifers up here produce pure clean air. By the time it drifts down to the valley floor, it is all used up and mixed up with all those pollutants. And, we have fresh spring water that feeds this small town that is perfect and pure."

I did not argue with that logic and look at more family photos in Lily's home office.

One must be of Lily as a young child standing with what must be her mother and father in front of a family home. Uncle Clint sees me looking at it and tells me about Lily's parents.

He begins, "Lily was only four in that photo and it was taken just before she lost them."

What!? I am shocked!

Clint sees my shock and explains.

"Lily's father was a detective in the bay area, and one morning as he and my sister were having breakfast before Lily's dad was to go to work, a man who her dad arrested and was later convicted, got out prison on parole, knocked on their door and shot her dad. He stepped into the house and killed my sister. The man then called the police from their home and went outside, sat on the front steps, and when the police arrived, he put the gun to his head and killed himself. The police found Lily upstairs under the covers of her bed. Terrified."

I stand in shocked disbelief!

Uncle Clint continues.

"So, that is how Lily came into Hazel's and my life. We couldn't have any kids of our own, and Lily was a blessing to Hazel and me. Thank goodness, her parents left her with some life insurance money so Lily was able to get a fine education. And after she graduated law school, Lily went to the police academy and followed her dad's footsteps in law enforcement."

My state of mind is locked into a trance as I listen to this horrible story.

And Lily's call for us to come to dinner, thankfully, awakens me from it. My nerves calm as Lily scolds us for being late in responding to her call to dinner and tells us that she was about to serve it to Sawdust and Cat. She is smiling as she speaks. Sawdust is at the screen door looking in. Sawdust is probably hoping that Lily will carry out her threat.

I sit at the table and Lily pours me a glass of iced tea, and I say, "Thank you, Sheriff."

"No, Glen, no," she says. "Tonight, would you please address me as Lily? But when we are around my deputies and staff, please address me as Sheriff."

Uncle Clint's mouth is filled with food, but he smiles his widest smile and lifts the one eyebrow much higher than the other again.

"Certainly." I pause briefly and then finish with, "Certainly, Lily!"

Now the food served at this table tonight is going to be even better than it already is!

This is a great meal of chicken and dumplings, homemade cornbread, turnip greens, and real mashed potatoes and dumpling gravy! When I complement Lily on her cooking, she passes the credit to Aunt Hazel, for it is Aunt Hazel's recipes that lend the delicious dishes their entire flavor.

We finish our meal and Lily shoos Uncle Clint and me out to the front porch and promises to bring out some fresh peach cobbler and a cold glass of milk. Oh, my, I am going to get a taste of the fruit of their peach tree after all!

We sit and wait for our peach cobbler.

Uncle Clint speaks first, as he usually does, and says, "Yes, Glen, Lily speaks about you every night, and not just about the case. She seems to be quite impressed with you, Glen."

"Oh, geez, Uncle Clint, this is not another one of your teases, is it? For I am quite impressed with Lily but do not dare go where my good senses tell me not to." I am surprised at myself for blurting out these words.

Uncle Clint laughs and says, "Oh, no, Glen, she really does speak highly of you, and that is the only reason that I invited you over tonight!"

I drop the matter and just sit and look down at Sawdust and Cat who have joined us on the porch. I scratch the ears on both of them, and I have immediately made two friends.

Lily soon brings out our peach cobbler, goes back inside, brings out another chair, sits and joins us with her own dish of peach cobbler and cold milk. What a perfect evening!

Uncle Clint has not finished his cobbler and milk, but he suddenly stands and heads down the porch steps. He calls back to us as he exits the gate.

"I'm headed down to the cafe and have a cup of coffee! Have a good night, Glen!"

I am too startled by his abrupt departure to politely return his good night, but Lily stands and calls out to him.

"Uncle Clint!" in her scolding voice, "You hardly ever go down to the cafe at this time of night! You come back here!"

But her words only hurry Uncle Clint's exit.

Lily and I sit awkwardly alone in each other's company as we finish our cobbler and milk.

I attempt to break the silence between us and ask, "How did Sawdust get his name?"

She welcomes the question with a sigh and says, "Uncle Clint found Sawdust when he was just a pup. Uncle Clint had gone out to the woodshed to get some wood for the fire and he was lying on a pile of sawdust. Uncle Clint brought him into the house so that we could warm him and the sawdust was still clinging to his fur. The sawdust stuck to him and so did the name!"

"And Cat?" I ask further.

"Cat showed up here one day. Neither of us wanted him so we never named him for fear that giving him a name might endear him to us. So, we just called him "Cat." But Cat would never leave, and eventually we accepted him as part of the family. As you can see, Cat and Sawdust are inseparable, and we just stuck with the name, Cat."

"Sawdust is a friendly dog," Lily continues. "He hardly ever barks and Cat seems to be infatuated with him."

Lily says further. "It is a strange relationship, but I have seen stranger."

The silence between Lily and I has been broken and she goes on with other stories about Uncle Clint and Aunt Hazel.

Again, it is a perfect evening of good food, good conversation, and good people.

Eventually Lily notices the late time and says that she needs to pick up the dishes and prepare to retire for the night.

But I have one more question.

Lily," I say. "I am concerned about what the professor gave to us and charged us with."

"Oh Glen, I know you are, and I share the same concerns. The promptings that the professor spoke of sometime overwhelm me and I do not know what to do about them."

Her response caught me off-guard and I reply, "I sense those same promptings and am worried about the cabin boy's secret log that is in your evidence room."

Lily stands up and says, "Come with me, Glen. Follow me, please."

I follow her to a hall\way door. She opens it and I follow her down a short flight of steps to a basement. She lifts a rug and underneath is the door of a safe. She dials a combination of numbers, turns the safe handle, reaches down and pulls up a heavy leather satchel! I step back suddenly without control.

She opens the heavy leather satchel and there it is!

The secret log of a young cabin boy.

I stand and stare at it, and my focus on it is intense, until I hear a soft cry coming from Lily!

I turn to her and there are tears flowing down her cheek!

She turns towards me, steps toward me and lays her face against my chest and softly cries.

I dare to fold my arms around her and hold her close and she begins to speak weakly and with regret! \.

"Oh Glen, I am so afraid that I have ignored my duty as sheriff. On that night that I dropped you off at your hotel, I intended to take this log to the evidence room but the promptings so overwhelmed me not to do so that I brought it here. And I have been so torn about what I have done that my mind has not allowed me any peace. I just need to know that I did the right thing!"

Oh, how I sense the turmoil that Lily is suffering. All I can do for the moment is hold her closer and let her sob out her concerns. After a few moments of embrace, a prompting causes me to ask, "Lily, you do understand that we must take this secret log to the mountain?"

"Yes, yes, Glen, I know," as she quietly regains control of her emotions.

And with that, she places the secret log back into the safe, and with hands clasped, we walk up the stairs, go into the kitchen and begin to pick up the dishes from the table. We work in quiet and happy unison together.

This is now a peaceful moment. But that is about to change!

A barking dog sounds an alarm!

"Lily," I say. "I thought you said that Sawdust hardly ever barks!"

She stops abruptly in her work at the kitchen counter and suddenly there is a yelp from Sawdust!

We both realize at the same moment.

There is someone inside the fence!

Lily's face has turned ashen, and I reach for one of the steak knives left on the kitchen table and open the back screen door.

No sooner than I open the screen door than a heavy stone fist crashes onto my temple. I am stunned, losing control as my knees begin to crumble.

Strong arms reach under my shoulder, prevent my falling. I am viciously shoved backwards and into one of the high-back kitchen chairs. Blurred visions of people entering the kitchen pass by my eyes!

It is Thor! And Lucas! And Felix!

Desperately, I try to hang on to my senses, but the heavy blow to my head has caused dizziness and my focus is difficult!

I see that they have forced Lily to sit in one of the kitchen chairs, and I realize that Thor is trying to speak to me.

"Wake up you stupid old fool!" He is yelling at me! "We're not going to kill you until you tell me what I want, but this pretty little Miss of yours might end up dead if you don't cooperate!"

They all have handguns and Lucas has his placed on Lily's head!

I stammer, "What is it you want?"

"You know what I want, Idiot! I want the damn signs!"

I am trying to think through the haze in my head!

I respond. "Okay, okay," I respond. "But do not hurt Lily!"

"Oh, so now she is Lily and not Sheriff! Oh, haven't you two gotten cozy! Well, Felix and Lucas here would like to get a little cozy with Lily and will have that chance before they kill her if you don't give me what I need!"

I desperately respond with, "I'll give what I know but I don't have the signs with me!"

What made me say that? Another prompting, I am sure!

"What in the hell do you mean?" asks Thor. "You don't have them with you?"

"I just can't remember them all but I have them written down in a notebook!"

"That is a damn lie! We were in your room and did not see any notebook!"

"Do you think I was stupid enough to leave them on the dresser top so you could walk in and pick them up?" I retort. "Now you are being an idiot!"

I continue.

"I had the hotel clerk put my notes in the hotel safe behind the lobby!"

Lily looks at me and there is anger in her face and her face also questions me as to what I just said!

Thor has a long pause.

"For some reason, I believe you, you old fool! Your feeble old brain probably couldn't retain all those signs, especially since your journal informed me about your brain injury you suffered in Viet Nam! 'Lost a little of your memory over there, did you?"

Thor believes my lie!

He calms and is thinking through his next steps.

"Okay, Lucas and I are going down to the hotel and Felix will keep you company. If it is not there, then your pretty sheriff is not going to be so pretty when Felix gets through with a little surgery on her face!"

Thor orders that we be tied up. Felix produces duct tape and secures us to the chairs.

Thor and Lucas begin to leave and Lucas finally speaks.

"Maybe we should bring him with us, Thor."

"No, if those deputies see him, they will be all over us. I am sure we can convince the clerk to open the safe."

Suddenly, I realize that I have exposed the hotel staff to great risks and regrets flood over my mind.

"Felix, if the old man here tries anything, cut the sheriff!" Thor's words chill my spine, for I have witnessed the cruelty of Felix!

Thor and Lucas leave the house!

No sooner than Thor and Lucas leave than Felix stands over Lily and looks down on her with a sinister smile.

Felix steps over to the kitchen table and begins to reach for one of the steak knives!

He is not going to wait for me to try anything and I am horrified!

Thor and Lucas had turned off the kitchen lights as they had left and only a faint beam of light trickles into the kitchen from the front room.

Just as Felix's hand was about to clutch the knife, a glint of light flashes across steel that crashes down on the hand of Felix. A chopping axe severs the fingers of Felix and four fingers are left on the table as Felix raises his hand in pain. With horror, he looks at the four bleeding stubs left on his hand!

With his other hand, Felix reaches for the hand gun he had placed on the table. This time the glint of a steel axe crashes into his skull and blood and other matter splatters across Lily's face and mine!

Felix's body thuds to the flood with a chopping axe imbedded in his skull and there are tanned and gnarled hands on the handle of the axe!

IT IS UNCLE CLINT!

There is a fire and rage in the eyes and face of Uncle Clint that cause him to be a man unknown to me before.

But as soon as he looks at his Lily, his eyes soften and tear up as he steps toward her, and holds her face in his hands. He sobs as he places his forehead on hers and cries out!

"Lily! Are you okay, my precious Lily!?!"

Lily and I struggle against our bound bodies, and soon Uncle Clint regains his composure and unties Lily first.

Lily is on the phone and calling the hotel to alert the deputies and hotel staff while Uncle Clint unties me.

Soon, there are sirens approaching the house and in moments there are blue and red flashing lights outside the house. Pounding footsteps are coming through the house as deputies pour in.

Lily is at once all business, and her concerns about the hotel staff and two deputies are relieved as a call confirms their safety.

Deputies are busy searching the immediate area around the house and going to all the rooms within the house. Lily is spending her time on the phone, and I can hear her calling out commands to search the hotel and all about it. Things are hurried, and I find a corner of the house where somehow, Sawdust and Cat are sitting and are evidently nervous about all the activity within the house.

Thank goodness that Sawdust and Cat are okay.

And then Lily's attention is turned to Uncle Clint.

He has been sitting on a kitchen chair with his head bent down and is trembling. He is in shock.

At this moment, he looks much older than his age. He looks like a broken and shivering man.

Lily tries to comfort him and orders a deputy to get paramedics in the house and take him to the hospital.

She asks for two deputies to accompany Uncle Clint

"We will go with him, Sheriff," says Deputy Bentley. "And we assure you, we will not leave his side."

Lily holds and comforts Uncle Clint until the paramedics arrive. They gently place the trembling old man onto a gurney and wheel him through the house and out of the front door.

I attempt to offer him a hand and well wishes, but his face is locked into a shivering trance. He does not hear my words of thanks and well wishes.

Lily goes with him to the waiting ambulance outside, and I hear her tell him that she will soon be to the hospital to check on him.

She comes back to the kitchen and sits on a kitchen chair. The body of Felix is lying at her feet.

Deputies are attempting to secure the crime scene. They ask me to take a seat in the front room. Sawdust and Cat move with me, and soon I see Detective Humphries arrive along another man in civilian clothes whom I have not met before. I soon overhear that he is the district attorney. I listen in on his conversation with Lily.

"Sheriff," he says. "I do not like doing this, but we have a problem here. We have a homicide in your home and from all accounts, your Uncle Clint committed this homicide. Now you know I am going to have to ask you to temporarily step aside from your office as sheriff until I can get an independent investigation that will clear you and Uncle Clint from any unlawful act. Sheriff Townsend?" He continues, "Are you going to have any difficulty with what I am saying?"

"No, Larry, I am not." Lily responds. "I understand."

"Sheriff," Larry continues. "I am going to have to ask you for your handgun and badge."

Lily reluctantly goes to her room and gets her badge and handgun.

Larry asks, "Is this your service issued handgun, Lily?"

"No, Larry," Lily says. "My serviced issued weapon is the armory down at the jail."

"Then this is your private weapon with all proper permits?" asks Larry.

"Yes," Lily responds again.

"Then your weapon is already secured in the armory. You keep this one, Lily."

Thank goodness! I think to myself. Common sense prevails up here in this rural county!

"Deputy Robinson!" Larry calls out.

A deputy steps forward and Larry speaks to him, "For the moment, Deputy Robinson, you are the senior deputy here, and you are now in charge of this scene!"

The deputy looks at Lily and is immediately apologetic. It is apparent that he assumes this new duty with reluctance. Lily offers words of confidence in him. Then she slumps down into one of the kitchen chairs, exhausted.

Both Lily and I are accompanied to the county jail by deputies. They bring Sawdust and Cat at the request of Lily.

I go to an interview room, and an interrogation from Detective Humphries and Detective Forman is conducted. After a brief explanation as to the event at Lily's home, and a few questions from the detectives, they send me to have a seat in the hallway. I wait. And I wait.

Eventually Lily and the detectives approach me, and Lily speaks.

"Mr. Becker. You, I, Sawdust and Cat are going to spend the night here at the jail. You will be placed in a cell but it will not be locked so as to allow you to use the facilities. Deputies will watch over all of us this night, so you should not have concerns about your safety. We regret this inconvenience, but considering all that has happened, we feel this is best."

"Yes, Sheriff, I understand but tell me, how is Uncle Clint?"

The sheriff says, "I spoke with Doctor Williams and he told me that Uncle Clint is suffering from shock, but will most likely recover rapidly. He is being kept overnight at the hospital. He has been given some sedatives. Knowing Uncle Clint, he will be wanting out of there very soon."

"Good!" I exclaim.

"Have a good night, Gl . . ." She hesitates and finishes with, "Mr. Becker."

"Thank you Sheriff." Lily and the detectives turn and head down the hallway.

I had noticed that Lily had a uniform on but without a badge. I assume they had taken the blue gingham dress, with Felix's blood and brain matter on it, into evidence, as they had taken my clothing with the same splattering and issued me a prisoner's uniform. It is difficult not to feel like a prisoner who is soon to be accompanied to a jail cell. But, oh, well. They assured me they would have clean clothes for me in the morning.

It was a fitful night of feigned sleep.

RETURN TO THE MOUNTAIN

There are no windows *in* this cell, so there is no morning sun to wake me. I miss the sun.

Activity in the jail has begun to increase, and I might as well get up and find a shower. Someone placed some clean clothes in my cell last night or this morning, so I must have dozed off and slept at least a little last night. I pick them up the clothes and step outside my cell. A deputy points the way to a shower. It is not nearly as private as the one in my hotel room, but the warm water is welcome as it pours over me. I almost feel invisible in the fresh clothes I put on, as compared to the orange jumpsuit that prisoners wear here in the jail.

I walk down the hallway in search of a break room that might have a coffee pot in it, and I notice Lily as she enters the building. No uniform this morning. She is wearing denim pants, boots, and a flannel shirt. She is dressed warmly this morning. It must be because of the cool mornings of late summer in the high country.

She notices me and approaches.

"Good morning, Mr. Becker," she calls out to me.

I greet her back and think how wonderful it is to see her this morning.

She disappears behind a door, and I stand just staring at the door, feeling disappointed. I had thought she was coming to speak with me. So, I continue my search for the break room and a cup of coffee. I think to myself, "Where was Lily at this morning? I thought she had stayed the night at the jail."

I continue my walk down the hall, and suddenly a small hand touches my backside. I turn and it is Lily!

My disappointment vanishes.

"Sheriff," I exclaim. "I thought you were staying in the jail last night."

"Oh, I did, but got up early, went home to clean up and put on some clean clothes, and now I am going to the hospital to check on Uncle Clint." Then, to my excitement, she adds, "I thought you might want to come along."

"I most definitely do, Sheriff," I respond.

And then she speaks in a low voice.

"You know you can call me Lily when we get out of here, don't you, Glen?"

My heart jumps, and I respond in a whisper, "Thank you, Lily."

She seems happy and excited this morning. I wonder how she possibly be so, after all that has happened. And then I recall the excitement and happiness I felt when I saw her. My mind is hoping for too much.

"Sheriff, where are Sawdust and Cat? If they spent the entire night here at the jail, should we take them out for a walk?' I ask.

"They are in my office and well cared for. The deputies brought in a litter box for Cat and both of them were taken out for several walks throughout the night. Everybody here thinks it is hilarious to watch them do their dance as they walk as Cat weaves through the legs of Sawdust. That darn Cat will not let Sawdust out of his sight, and all the deputies love walking them! They all want their turn. Lily laughs as she tells me of these things.

"We are walking to the hospital." Lily tells me and directs me to the door.

Two great stone sphinxes walk just to the rear of us.

We enter the hospital and stop.

The lobby is filled with people. Then we realize why.

Professor Shumway's family is here in great numbers.

They see us and begin to approach and extend their expressions of gratitude over again for they have happy news. The professor's recovery is going quite well, and all have just been told that he could be released from the hospital in just a few days and transferred to a nursing facility in the Bay Area. Even better, he should not have to be in the nursing facility for very long. There is a party atmosphere in the lobby, and I can see that Lily is very much pleased with the news, as am I!

Finally, we politely excuse ourselves and begin to walk towards the elevators. I stop and Lily looks at me.

"Sheriff," I say. "I need to speak with you in private, for just a few minutes. Could we please go to the cafeteria and perhaps have a cup of coffee?"

She pauses and then says, "Yes, of course, Mr. Becker." And we head in the direction of the cafeteria.

We enter and she asks the deputies to please allow us some space so we can speak privately.

They do, and as we go through the line, I sweeten my coffee and add a bit cream. She drinks her coffee black and passes by the condiment table and finds a table in the corner. We sit.

"What is it, Glen?" she asks.

"Lily, I know where that white pinnacle of rock is that sits in front of dark gray granite cliffs."

She sits in silence and knows I want to continue.

I continue.

"A lot of Sierra trekkers know where that rock is, and many have their photos taken as they stand beside it. But there is no opening on the cliffs behind it, and it is difficult to believe the professor and the cabin boy's story. But I sense that we must both there go there soon and take the secret log with us."

Her response is anticipated, but still surprising.

"Darn these promptings that I feel, Glen. I have been prompted that you know where the white pinnacle of rock is and that it is time to take the secret log to the site. I do not understand where all these promptings come from, but that is why I am dressed the way I am. We are going there, with the secret log, after we see Uncle Clint."

We sit and stare at one another. Lily reaches her hand out to touch mine and we catch the deputies looking at us. They politely turn their heads and she quickly withdraws her hand. We have been caught, but something tells me that the deputies respect what is occurring between Lily and me. The something is a prompting! What are these promptings and where do they come from?"

Lily and I get up from our table and head towards the elevators to Uncle Clint's room. We exit the elevators, turn down the hallway, and hear a woman's laughter coming from a room. There are two deputies standing at the doorway.

"Oh my!" exclaims Lily, as she smiles. "Who is Uncle Clint teasing now?"

We look into the doorway and it is Nurse Nancy standing at the foot of Uncle Clint's bed enjoying good laughs and the company of Uncle Clint.

"Uncle Clint!" Lily calls out. "What have you done that I will have to apologize to Nancy for?"

Nurse Nancy catches her breath and says, "Oh, Sheriff. You be polite towards your uncle! His remarks to me are private, and although I would never repeat them in public, this is the best company of a man that I have had in a long time. So you leave him be, and don't you scold him!" With that, she leaves the room with a laugh and an admonishment to Lily, "Now you be nice to that uncle of yours, you hear?"

Uncle Clint is doing quite well.

Uncle Clint's smile and lifted eyebrow that he cast at us is contagious again. It is good to be happy.

"How are you doing, Glen?" Uncle Clint calls out.

"Well, obviously I am not dong as well as you," I laughingly respond.

"Lily! How are you doing?" Uncle Clint inquires.

"Besides having to apologize for your behavior, I am just fine!" laughs Lily.

"Come on over here girl and let me hug you." Uncle Clint's invitation for a hug is welcomed, and Lily approaches him with welcome arms.

He embraces her and then speaks as he swings his legs out of the bed and starts to get up.

"Now, Lily," he says. "Get me outta here!"

She pushes him on the chest and sits him back down on the bed.

"You are not going anywhere until the doctor releases you, so you just lie back down and wait!" Lily's words are firm and without humor.

He sits up on his bed, folds his arms tightly and frowns.

"Uncle Clint, you sit there. We need to talk, and we need your help." Lily firmly says.

Uncle Clint's entire mood changes and he looks seriously at Lily's face.

He is receiving a prompting!

Uncle Clint speaks. "What do the two of you need and what are you doing?"

"Uncle Clint," Lily says softly. "Do you know of a white pinnacle of rock upon the mountain that stands out from all the dark granite cliffs at the mountain's peak?"

Uncle Clint does not answer quickly, but waits and measures the seriousness of Lily's question. Then he responds.

"Every old-timer in this town has been to that rock at least a few times when they were younger. But, why would you be interested in that rock?"

There is caution and concern in his voice.

Lily answers his question. "This is a time in which you need to trust Glen and me and believe there is reason for us to go to that white pinnacle. There is a purpose peculiar to a unique situation that Glen and I have been chosen for, and we know that we do this for good cause."

Lily's words fill me a sense that there is something upon her that is beyond mortal explanation. Something spiritual. And I have not used that word, spiritual, since vacation bible school as a child.

Lily continues. "Glen and I are going to that white pinnacle, and we need you to know that if we do not return soon, we will be in the area of the white pinnacle."

Uncle Clint does not respond but I sense that promptings are pouring out upon him.

He finally responds. "You go there and do what you are being called upon to do, but know this. If the two of you are not back by late afternoon, this whole county will be searching for you."

He continues.

"Go now! And watch over one another and return to me safely."

Uncle Clint calls out to me as we approach the door. "Glen. You bring my Lily home safe!"

I nod my head, yes, and Lily and I leave.

The mountain looms above us as we exit the hospital entrance door. It seems of greater heights than ever before.

THE MUSEUM

We stand at the hospital exit and I ask, "Lily, how are we going to excuse these two deputies and get away from them?"

The deputies overhear my questions and are startled.

Lily responds. "Excuse me, Glen, wait here." Lily calls the deputies over to walk with her, and they leave my range of being able to hear their conversation.

There appears to be an argument among the three of them. Words are exchanged, and the deputies seem to be protesting Lily's words.

Eventually, Lily prevails and the deputies turn down the sidewalk and begin to walk away.

Lily returns to my side and says, "For the moment, I may not be their sheriff, but they respect me as Lily and will leave us to ourselves for a few hours."

What a person and a woman, I think to myself as we go on our way.

We get into Lily's SUV that was parked in the hospital lot. Lily says we need to stop by her house.

We park in the back yard, enter the house, and head directly down to the basement to recover the heavy leather satchel and secret log of the young cabin boy.

On our way out, we grab some bottled water and throw it into a backpack that Lily had. I have the heavy leather satchel on my backside. We get into the SUV, and Lily says to me, "Show me where to go."

We start out, and I tell her that we will go to some four-wheel drive trails that will get us within trekking distance of the white pinnacle. As we drive along the trails, I point out the different points of forks and trails that we should take; Darn, I hope my memory is serving me correctly.

It is slow going as the four-wheel drive trails begin to narrow and become more demanding, but the promptings that are upon us both are guiding us as much as my memory—just as the promptings helped guide Drake and the young cabin boy to the pinnacle.

We finally reach the point at which we must begin to trek.

I think what a difficult trip this is, and then I remember the difficult trek of the young cabin boy and Drake, and I am humbled.

We park the SUV under a huge tree and load our backs with our cargo.

We look upward.

My God! The great peaks of the Sierras have never looked so high!

I look at Lily, and there is nothing but determination and beauty upon her face.

And we begin our ascent.

Just as Drake and the young cabin boy, we are guided by promptings, so much clearer than my remembrance of the location of the great white pinnacle.

We struggle through the great forests and over streams and obstacles that seem to want to throw both of us back on the valley floor. But we continue, and the fatigue that would normally have already deprived my older body of continuance is not present. We are both energized by a sense of higher calling than our bodies would have otherwise been capable of.

The heavy leather satchel on my backside is lightened by the sense of closeness of our objective.

We rest for a moment.

Lily is looking at me, and her breath gasps for the thin oxygen that is rare at this altitude.

She is more alive than at any time I have ever seen her, and she is beautiful.

We turn our heads towards the summit, and we get up, and push on.

We are there!

We both rest with our hands extended up on the white pinnacle of rock.

Our breath is heavy and our lungs are sucking in all the oxygen that is left at this altitude.

Our gaze is upon each other, and we are filled with anticipation at what we mind find as we are near the completion of our duty that the professor charged us with.

Finally, we drop our hands from the white pinnacle, approach one another and embrace!

And we embrace with an effect that goes beyond mortal comprehension of affection for one another.

I have never experienced such glorious affection! And I am happy beyond belief!

And then, practicality and purpose of mind grips us, and we continue our most understood mission . . . to deliver the secret log of the young cabin boy.

Why?

The reason for delivery of this secret log has not yet been realized to either of us, but we know we must do so.

We gather our senses and step behind the white pinnacle of rock and look at one another again. We drop to our knees, look upon the great dark granite cliffs and begin to sign.

We exhibit the signs that the professor had taught us to repetitively do over and over again. We do so in perfect unison.

And as we rise, our eyes are wide open and we watch as the granite seems to disappear as if a great veil of granite had lifted. It opened, and a great opening that had not been present before, suddenly appears and a glow of light from within illuminates its entrance. A welcoming of entry is prompted from within us!

Together, Lily and I begin our entrance into the great opening. Within a few steps of our entry, I feel a hard press upon the base of my skull that is the cold hard steel of a weapon within the grip of Thor!

Immediately, I look at Lily and there is a startled look of her face, and she too, has a muzzle of steel pressed against her that is gripped by Lucas!

Our bliss of the moment is horridly interrupted by two missionaries of death!

The next words are uttered by Thor. "Polite words cannot express my appreciation for opening this vault, Mr. Becker! So, to hell with politeness and go forth and let's see what we might find, or Lucas might find personal pleasure with your friend!"

"You two wore us out with your hurried rush up here, so we might find a place to pause and find use of your pretty friend if you do not co-operate, Mr. Becker, so please continue on and see what we might find!"

Thor's mouth is filthy, and I find his threats to be abhorrent and disgusting! But, I pause, look at Lily and see defiance in her eyes and deliberately step forward.

We move on and there ahead of us is a glow of light upon an object sitting upon a pillar of rock that seems to be coming from a source that I cannot identify.

It is the golden text, brought here by Drake and the cabin boy!

Its golden bindings and golden pages are illuminated by light that seems to have no source.

I look above the great walls of this tomb and see no cracks in its ceiling or no source of outside light. Where does this source of light come from except from within the great vault self?

I do not know!

Thor also sees the golden text, and as I glance backwards at him, his eyes glisten brightly with unrighteous greed and excitement!

The muzzles of steel are pressed tightly against Lily's and my skulls; but, as their greed intensifies, Thor's and Luca's grips loosen and they step forward ahead of us and approach the golden text we know was left here by Drake.

They stand in front of it and are amazed by its glory in its self-illuminating light.

They seem to about ready to reach out and grasp it and I call out to them to stop.

Thor looks back, lifts his weapon and says, "I don't need you anymore, Idiot!" But before he can fire his weapon, Lily throws her body between Thor and me and absorbs the bullet intended for me!

She crumbles into my arms and Thor laughs out loud! He laughingly mocks the cruelty of his act and speaks to me.

"Oh, this is good! This is even better! Now you can watch her die!"

I catch Lily's dying body in my arms, and we watch as Thor reaches for the golden text.

But before he can grasp it, a bright illuminated figure of a man, clothed in beautiful white garments, who is seemingly floating slightly above us, speaks out these words to Thor! His voice is as the roar of a mighty lion that asserts its authority over all those who threaten his pride!

"No unclean hands shall touch these precious things of the Great Father, so stand back, and depart this holy place!"

Thor is shocked at the presence of such of a being and the words spoken by him, but Thor's greed overcomes his momentary pause and he reaches out for the golden text!

It will be his last greedy outreach!

Thor's hand almost reaches the golden text!

But, before his last greedy grasp . . .

His hand begins to darken and almost immediately begins to smolder! His arm begins to darken, and the smoldering continues upward into his arm, his shoulder and then into his face!

Thor's entire face is smoldering with the burning of flesh, and a look of terror is upon his face as Lily and I realize that the last look upon Thor's face, at his dying moment, was one of looking upon the very face of Satan and into the very horror of Hell!

Thor collapses into a pile of ashes at the foot of the pillar of stone that supports the golden text.

Lily's life is fading from her body and I hold her tightly to me!

Lucas has been petrified at the sight of Thor's burning flesh and he turns to run to the exit of the great vault of the Sierras, but before he can reach the exit, another bright illuminated figure of a woman appears before him, reaches out her hand and places it on Lucas's forehead. His face begins to darken and turn to ash and his body of flesh burns and falls into smoldering soot at the foot of the illuminated figure clothed in brilliant white garments.

Who are these illuminated persons dressed in brilliant white?

I turn my attention to Lily, and blood is leaking from her precious body and beginning to cake and grow dark on her clothing. Her eyes are dimming, and her breathing is heavy as she is losing her life to great injury.

We are looking into one another's eyes and she is weakening with every moment of her last breaths of life.

And then the illuminated man dressed in brilliant white clothing speaks out to us.

"Reach out the hand of Lily and place it upon the golden text," He says in a strong but kind voice.

I look at him with horror in my heart upon hearing his words for I have just witnessed the burning of Thor after he had attempted to grasp the golden text.

The brilliant figure hears my thoughts, although they have not been spoken, and speaks again.

"Her heart is pure, and her hands are clean of evil. Know that the Father intends no harm towards her."

I look at Lily and there is ascent in her eyes towards my placing of her hand on the golden text.

The brilliant figure speaks again.

"Hold out her hand on the golden text and witness the power and mercy of your Great Father!"

I grasp Lily's arm with great trepidation and stretch it out towards the golden text. Her hand falls upon the golden text.

My eyes close as I do so!

A feeling of life is suddenly growing in Lily and startles my eyes open.

I look upon her, and color is returning to her face and her breathing is relaxed! Her face and eyes are beginning to glow with energy and new life! Her caking blood on her clothing is beginning to be cleansed, and even the hole left by the bullet in her clothing is mending. She is aglow with life!

I am so weakened with happiness and amazement that I can hardly hold her as she reaches her arms around my neck. We embrace one another while sobbing on to each other's shoulder, great tears of joy at the return of life to her once dying body!

We look up at the brilliant figure and are stunned with amazement and gratitude at the brilliant figure. We are in awe and wonder, "Who are these seemingly angels?

I begin to regain my strength and Lily and I embrace each other as the two brilliant figures move towards each other's side, clasp hands, smiles upon us, and then, the brilliant man speaks to us!

"Your Father is grateful that you have brought to Him a great artifact that is precious to Him and is a testament of Him and His great plan!"

He continues.

"The witness of record, that the young cabin boy of Sir Francis Drake wrote, will be preserved in this Holy Temple and Museum. Know that the Father holds many artifacts of record that testify of His good plan and He keeps them here for a special day when they will be lifted up along with all His good people on that great day which only the Father knows! Walk now, through this Holy Museum, and witness those things that are precious to the Lord. Then return to us for further revelation!"

Lily and I look at one another, and as our stunned minds begin to return to our senses, look out beyond the golden text and see other artifacts resting upon stone pillars. All that we see is illuminated by the strange, but beautiful, light that seems to come from within them.

We walk along a path towards them. There are many to behold in this great cavernous room ahead of us.

We come upon a pillar of rock that has upon it a chalice. And a prompting comes upon us that it is the one of the Last Supper of Christ with his disciples!

And then we see a crown of thorns that was cruelly placed upon the head of Christ. And beside it, a dove, gilded in gold that is holding an olive branch that is also gilded in gold and after that, a staff. The staff of Moses that struck open the Red Sea that allowed his people to pass. The same staff that was later struck upon a desert rock and brought forth water to give drink to his people. The same staff that once turned into a great snake that devoured the snakes of a pharaoh's priests!

We witness a long list of many other things of great biblical accounts that include the sling of David that brought down Goliath and many other things that have never been accounted for by archaeology and other sciences. There is an ugly and gruesome scourge that still has the stains of Christ's blood on its many horrid tentacles!

We pass by many other artifacts too numerous to count. We are in awe in all that we see.

And then we enter a great room. We walk in and see a great wooden boat of large dimension.

The ark of Noah! That great ship that carried Noah and his family and all the animals over the waters of the great flood!

At last, Lily and I bow our heads and walk humbly back towards the brilliant figures.

They greet us with gracious smiles. And he speaks!

"Know that these are all things of record that the Father holds dear to Him! And there will be more that will be brought here, for His great works continue, and they will be received with great respect and watched over so as no unclean thing shall touch them!"

He continues, as he reaches out his hand to grasp the brilliant woman's hand beside him.

"My eternal companion and I will be called for other work of the Father one day. On that day, the two of you will be called forth to watch over these precious things of the Father. A promise is made to you that the joy you will experience together here will be a thousand-fold greater than what you are now going to enjoy as eternal companions in the many years of mortal life that lie before you! Go forth now, and never speak of these things you have witnessed here until the Holy Prompter calls upon you to do so."

As he finishes, a prompting begins to overwhelm me. I look at Lily and I know she has the same prompting. I ask, as the words almost choke my throat, "Drake? Sir Francis Drake? Are you Sir Francis Drake?"

The brilliant figure responds.

"It matters not what my mortal name is. Know that there are many who will be called upon to perform a calling of the Father that is beyond mortal comprehension. When called upon, place your faith above your mortal concerns and witness the blessings of the Father! Go now, and enjoy your eternal companionship. Keep a pure heart and clean hands."

Lily and I are in awe and look at one another, join hands, and leave the brilliant couple behind us as we exit the Holy Temple and Museum's great granite doors.

We step out into bright Sierra sun, and the veil of granite reappears and seals the temple doors behind us.

Together, we step upon a huge fallen granite boulder. We look down upon the fallen granite underneath the great cliffs as the forest edge beckons us to begin our descent.

We look down upon the forest's edge, and there emerging from the forests, far beneath us, is Uncle Clint! And deputies are also along the forest's edge. Sawdust and Cat are bounding up as granite stones toss about behind them.

Uncle Clint and the deputies are opening their arms and waving up to us.

Lily steps off the great boulder and on down to the next. Soon Sawdust and Cat are the first to greet her. The rest are soon to be next to her with warm hugs and greetings. All are happy and it is a glorious scene that is unfolding beneath me.

I stand atop the great rock, hold my head up to a clear blue sky, thrust my arms up open wide and call out to the Sierra heavens!

Ah!!! The ambiance!!!

The End

ABOUT THE AUTHOR

The author is of Louisiana birth and was reared in a sparsely populated area of Southwest New Mexico, in the high country of the Gila and Apache National Forests. His attraction to the high country was interrupted by his call to duty in the Viet Nam War and the ordeal of ordinary life in seeking means so as to raise his family. The author's attempt at this novel is tempered by personal experiences.

His hope is that all readers will attempt to relate to other readers their personal experiences by interlacing them with their hopes and aspirations. Good reading to all!

ABOUT THE BOOK

Glen's quiet and peaceful retirement is rudely interrupted when he interferes with the torture of an innocent victim by three assailants. His involvement casts him into an adventure of intrigue and treasure, along with Lily, the town sheriff, that will test their faith and character and lead them into a relationship that is as surprising as it is wonderful. Their response to a call of duty will place not only them in danger, but it also threatens the lives of all of those who they care for. Walk with them and see how ordinary people may be called upon to perform extraordinary events.